GIDDY UP, Gorgeous

CASSANDRA JOELLE

For I know the plans I have for you," declares the Lord, "plans to prosper you and not to harm you, plans to give you hope and a future.
Jeremiah 29:11 NIV

CHAPTER 1

Sadie

The best thing about being an actress, by far, was the "glam squad" that came to my condo to get me ready for events. After my role in last summer's blockbuster film, *All Bets on Him,* about a professional poker player turned ranch owner, my phone had not stopped ringing since. I thanked God every day for the gifts He had given me.

I'd just been informally offered a role in another big film yesterday. It was going to be filmed on location in Australia in three months, and I was going to be taking on the role of a surfer who had a near-miss with a shark. Sure, it had been done, but this angle felt fresh, since the shark was also missing most of its teeth due to an unknown accident. *Gummy, The Great White* would be a dark comedy thriller. All glory to God.

Quite possibly the most exciting thing that had happened this month was meeting Tommy Wheeler in the waiting room of my agency. He was Hollywood's darling, playing a cowboy in the number one television show in the country, for three seasons. There had been rumors that it was about to be renewed for another five seasons, just like that. He was so good at what he did, that he started dressing the part all the time. Never coming out of character. While I'd only known him as a cowboy, it was hard to see him playing the role of anything else.

As I sat in the "glam chair," the glam squad was putting curlers in my hair while I recounted meeting Tommy. My best friend, Molly, was the first one I called after meeting him.

"You'll never guess who I just met," I said, breathless from the adrenaline of a new connection.

"Leo? Ricky Martin? The Backstreet Boys!?"

"No way. I don't even know how I'd meet them," I said, suddenly feeling like this wasn't as exciting in comparison. "This man and I—our agents work for the same place."

"Hmm. I don't know then. Just tell me, already!"

"Tommy Wheeler," I said, followed immediately by her gasps and screams. Once she calmed down, she got straight to the point.

"Okay," she said, breathless. "Start from the top. What were you doing? What were you wearing? And what was the exact prayer you prayed this morning?"

"Molly," I laughed, rolling my eyes.

"No, no. I'm not kidding. I need the syntax. Was it formal? Casual? Any certain phrases repeated with holy emphasis?"

A large cloud of hair spray dropped down over me, and I held my breath. "Sorry," Tricia, one of my glam squad, said. "That's probably the last of the hairspray. I just need to use the spray adhesive on your dress straps and no more aerosols." I nodded, thanking her.

"Not so fast," Brittany said. "I need to do her setting spray for her makeup and body bronzer." She grinned, holding up a giant can to my face. "But this is at least pleasant, more of a spritz of air, and I'm pretty sure it's non-toxic," she winked.

"Pretty sure?" I asked, with a cocked eyebrow.

"No sudden movements just yet. You're wearing enough makeup that it's working as a mask until I use this." I closed my eyes just in time for her to start shellacking my face with the fresh scented spray. A giddy feeling ran through my veins.

"I'm so excited," I said under my breath. Brittany agreed.

"You are going to have the best time tonight. I can't wait to see photos of you and Tommy dressed to the nines," she gushed. Just the thought of my handsome *boyfriend* gave me butterflies.

When my agent had called me in for a meeting a few weeks ago, she said there was someone she wanted me to meet. So, when I walked into the waiting room, and I saw a gorgeous man in a cowboy hat, my heart leapt. I assumed she was talking about him. He looked me up and down and walked right over to me, not even bothering to introduce himself, which I'd found out was a habit of his. He liked to say, "Why tell them what they already know?" It was true; everyone who wasn't living under a rock knew who Tommy Wheeler was. Heck, he played Ford McCallum. If they didn't call him Tommy, they called him Ford. He answered to both.

When I met him, I immediately thought of a recent interview that he did for a western magazine that was splashed all over the internet. The interviewer had asked him what the most important thing in his life was. You know what he said? His faith in God. I knew our values aligned perfectly, because I felt the exact same way. Tommy was ten years older than me. I was mostly shocked that he was even single when he asked me out to dinner upon meeting. I immediately accepted, admittedly feeling a little starstruck by him. He was just so handsome in his cowboy hat and jeans.

Now, we'd been on several dates. He took me out every weekend when he was back from filming in Texas. It was a part of his contract to be home on the weekends, and since he was the biggest star on the show, they aimed to please him.

This would be our public debut as a couple. Tommy made sure that I knew that. When he asked if I wanted to attend with him, he implied that it was a really big deal.

"You know what this means, don't you?" he asked. I shrugged.

"That people will know we've been dating?"

"That we are a real couple now. And this is one of the things that real couples do together." I smiled.

"Does this mean we are boyfriend and girlfriend?" I asked. He shrugged and nodded.

"I mean, yeah, it does." Wow. Tommy Wheeler was my *boyfriend!*

Now, as the glam squad glued my western leather fringe dress straps to my shoulders, doing a quick "pull test" to see if there was any movement, I let out a scream, as I was certain they'd removed some of my skin.

"Don't worry," Tricia consoled me. "This is water soluble." I looked down at my gown.

"Does that mean I have to shower with this thing on to remove the straps?" Tricia looked lost in thought.

"You know, when you asked me to make sure there was no slippage with these heavy, loose straps, I didn't think of that." It was true—a wardrobe malfunction was my worst nightmare. I didn't care if any jewels fell off or a button popped. But losing my sense of modesty in front of everyone? No thank you.

This dress was already pushing my limits, but Tommy said it was important that I dressed "the part" of his date. Because he was wearing a Stetson, a bolero, and custom alligator boots, that meant I needed to be dressed like a western woman. Never mind that I was up for best supporting actress for my movie, Tommy was nominated for seven awards total. His night was "more important," as he kept telling me. Which, yes, was rude. But, I understood that. Besides, I wanted to stand by his side more than I did receive an award. It was just the plain truth. I was thrilled to be his girl.

"So," Brittany said, lowering her voice so others wouldn't hear as they packed up their train cases of makeup products that transformed me into a western Barbie. "What parties will you be attending tonight?" She took a large wooden brush with soft, wide bristles and brushed it through my blonde curls, leaving a soft shimmer of glitter in its wake. Brittany loved celebrity gossip, as I always overheard her filling in her coworkers on things which wasn't so great in this industry. Last month, she prepped me for a television interview, and I heard her tell Tricia that so-and-so had to wax her forearms because they had such natural, dark hair, but it was really her bad breath that was the biggest problem for her co-stars. I'd always kept a tight lip around her, and if she ever tried to tell me anything, I waived it off like I was not interested. But in this case, I really had no idea.

"Wherever Tommy wants to go, I suppose," I said, with an honest shrug. She raised her eyebrows and gave me a sideways smile.

"Well, do tell, next time I see you," she said. Thankfully, all I had left to do was put on my turquoise and diamond jewelry, on loan from a very famous designer from Rodeo Drive. She let out a low whistle as she stepped back.

"Sadie Clark—I do say—you look spectacular." I turned around in my chair and took in my full reflection in one of the many mirrors in my dressing room. The entire second bedroom of my apartment had been converted into my vanity, something I still hadn't gotten comfortable with, but according to my manager, this was the way it was.

My shoulder-length, blonde hair was in a soft curl style, clipped around my hairline with discreet bobby pins. It had a peach hue to it, my natural blonde tone, and tonight, it shimmered from whatever product Brittany added into it with the brush. I felt like a fairy. My makeup was done up as much as I'd ever seen it—smokey, eyeliner rimmed eyes made my brown eyes look hard. Light lipstick made my full lips nearly blend into my makeup. Copious amounts of bronzer made it look like I'd been living in St. Tropez, not in an apartment in Los Angeles. They kept telling me how beautiful I looked, and I did feel that. There was no denying that they did a great job on my look tonight. But there was something about wearing a fresh face, no stitch of makeup in sight, that made me feel the most like myself.

The dress fit like a glove. Coming right to my ankles, the slit up my left leg stopped right above the knee, thanks to a safety pin. It was still cute without it coming up to my underwear, I decided. The long pieces of fringe around the dress made me feel glamorous but also created a slapping sound when I walked. I thought, *Maybe it would be better if I walked slower.* So, I practiced walking in slow motion around my condo, and I looked insane. *Better to look insane than the sound of slapping someone across the face?* Debatable.

Though it didn't technically show cleavage or anything *risqué*, it was still awfully tight. I felt like it wasn't as modest as it could have been, but Tommy picked it out and insisted I would match him perfectly in it. My boots sat by the door. They were custom leather cowboy boots, taken from the measurements of my bare foot, and bedazzled. Originally, they went over the knee, but I changed them to mid-calf, because the former didn't feel practical with the improved slit of the dress.

While I looked pretty, I didn't feel like myself. All of this makeup made me look older than I was. And heck, I was young. Only twenty-four years old, but I did feel wise beyond my years. I knew what this was and what it wasn't. This industry wanted me to look a certain way. Everything was curated. But I didn't want to ever lose myself because nothing was worth that.

"I can do the rest myself," I said, much to Brittany's disappointment. As much as she loved her job, I could tell that the gossip was her favorite part, and she shrugged when she knew, once again, I wasn't going to give her anything to talk about.

"Alright, then. Don't forget your boots have that inside zipper if you can't fit your ankle in." I nodded, thankful for the reminder.

After she left my apartment, and I heard the elevator ding as she walked inside the doors, I took a deep breath, locking the door behind me.

All of my jewelry was sitting on a black velvet tray. There was a set of dazzling earrings—two pear-cut diamonds, trickling down with turquoise cabochons set in the brightest, white gold I've ever seen. Each earring felt like a brick hanging from my lobe. Thankfully, they were clip-ons. If only they made push up bras for ears. I could certainly be a candidate, if only to take the weight off my earlobes for the evening.

The ring was a multi-faceted diamond in a thick, white gold band with a turquoise inlay. It was a stunning piece, but it only fit on my left ring finger. My right ring finger was jammed in a bike accident as a kid and was always a little bit rounder than the other. For a moment, I considered not wearing the diamond ring, as the implications of that were wild, but then I decided because it went with the set, I would be crazy not to.

Lastly, a large, squash blossom necklace finished off the look, pairing perfectly with my leather dress. Small diamonds were faceted around the heavy turquoise. Together, despite the jewelry weighing me down, it looked incredible.

Sliding into my boots, I nearly forgot about the zipper as I struggled to get my ankle through them, when I remembered. My dress was so tight, I was having a hard time bending over in the dress. There wasn't much stretch to the leather, something I wish I had realized before I agreed to wear this. The thought of winning my award for best supporting actress flashed through my mind: What if I couldn't make it up the stairs to accept my award?

For custom boots, they sure weren't comfortable. I'd rather have been wearing a pair of stiletto heels tonight than this. My phone alarm went off; my driver would be here in ten minutes. Tommy would already be in the car. My cheeks flushed at the thought. This was the only alone time I was going to have tonight, and I was ready to say my prayers. I was certainly going to need them.

Dear God,

Thank You for bringing me here tonight. May Your glory shine through me, Lord. Do not let the enemy distract me from You. Lord, help me keep Your virtues. Help me stay on the path of righteousness. May I bring You honor in everything I do.

In Your name,

Amen.

The moment I was done praying, my phone rang. I sat still for a moment, feeling like I hadn't had a chance to relish in my prayer for long enough yet. Hesitantly, I reached for the phone. It was my manager, Janie. I answered.

"Hey, Janie."

"Sadie!" Her voice was high and shrill.

"What's wrong?" I asked, standing up.

"Nothing is wrong. Everything is right!" I let out a sigh of relief, mixed with laughter.

"You scared me there for a second."

"Guess who wants YOU to be the leading lady in *Cue the Night?*" My heart dropped. That was a role I was hesitant to audition for because it was a movie about vampires. The more I prayed about it, the stronger my conviction grew against it.

"Well, I'm flattered, but I'm going to have to decline." Janie let out a gasp, followed by a whine. I'm sure her commission on that would have been great.

"What do you mean?" she demanded.

"I don't want to glorify demons. I'm sorry, Janie. I shouldn't have auditioned for it. That was a waste of everyone's time."

"But you wouldn't be glorifying them. You'd be slaying them—oh wait, I'm getting another call. Ugh. I have to take this. You know what? Let's sleep on it. Have fun tonight. I hope you win. Call me tomorrow when you wake up and we can have a real chat. Buh-bye." She ended the call before I could remind her that tomorrow was Sunday. Other than church, I needed the day to lay low and not be worshipping my work schedule. Janie was notoriously unaccepting of a first response, but I knew she would come around. At the end of the day, I was the one steering my career, and I wanted to do it with God in mind.

I was off to a great start. From my last movie, I paid off my parents' house. I bought this condo in the middle of the city. There was a palm tree out my window and a private pool for my leisure. Sure, I had very little left over to show for it. But my phone was ringing off the hook with more offers every day. Things had only increased since I started being associated with Tommy. And just as I thought of his name, my door buzzer went off. He was here, and the night was young.

CHAPTER 2

Sadie

"You look like a rodeo queen," Tommy whispered into my ear and kissed my cheek as the limousine door shut behind me. The driver, Pete, made his way to the front. Tommy hit the privacy button, and a partition went up between us. My cheeks reddened.

"Thank you. Isn't that a line from your show?" I teased. I knew it wasn't. I'd watched every episode, which was not hard to do as it was always on. Tommy shook his head.

"No. But if it is, it's because I'm going off the cuff a lot of the time. The director lets me improvise. The character is written about me, after all." We may have been dating for just three weeks, but I'd already heard this speech a few times. I just nodded. He put his arm around me, and I got my first glimpse at his outfit. He was wearing a suit but with a bolero, like he said. His signature cowboy hat looked out of place in the limo.

"You look nice," I said. "I've not seen you in anything other than jeans yet." Tommy rolled his eyes.

"The stylist had a cow when I told her I just wanted to wear my Wranglers. She said even cowboys have to dress up once in a while." I let out a laugh. "What's so funny?"

"Nothing." But I couldn't hold back my laughter. "It's just that... You're from Malibu. This role... It's just that... You're playing a part. You're not *actually* a cowboy." His face went red, as he removed his arm from my shoulders.

"And you're not a cowgirl." He crossed his arms. What was happening here?

"I know I'm not. You told me to wear this, remember? I wanted to wear a pink jumpsuit with sparkly shoes." He rolled his eyes. Again. Uh oh. Had the night already gone sour?

Tommy was my first real boyfriend. Aside from a brief courtship that ended before it started, I decided to wait until I felt ready to date for marriage to start, which wasn't until well after high school. I was so lanky, nerdy, and had big braces on my teeth until my senior year, that I didn't have my radar on boys hardly at all. My parents used to tell me it was better to be a late bloomer, and truthfully, I had always been settled on the path that the Lord had for me. I just knew that one day, I would meet my perfect prince charming. I never wanted to date around to find him. And I was so thankful that I met Tommy. Though I didn't like how he was acting, Tommy might have still been my perfect guy. Because this was the fairytale I had always wanted to get.

I was far from Tommy's first girlfriend. While I hadn't looked up his dating history that I could surely have found out from an internet search, I had decided early on that I would have just made myself mad with jealousy if I did. No, it was much better to take his word for it. He had mentioned a few women that he'd dated in the past, and they were all famous actresses and names that I recognized, but I never pressed for more information. I just didn't want to know the nitty gritty details.

My phone buzzed inside my small purse. I peeked inside, considering Tommy was now ice cold to me anyway. It was Molly.

Molly: How's the limousine? Do you feel like a Hollywood Barbie? Remember that Barbie limousine we had when we were little that had the hot tub in the back? Imagine being stuck in traffic whilst sitting in your limousine hot tub. If the smog didn't get you first, pruning in the tub might.

Sadie: I may have accidentally told him he's not a real cowboy.

Molly: ...Oh no. You bruised the Hat Ego.

Molly was right, per usual. But now what? Before I could decide, the limo came to a stop. We were here, and Tommy and I hadn't reconciled from whatever disagreement we just had. Here was our red carpet debut as a couple. I took a deep breath as the door swung open. Tommy slid out, but not before putting my hand in his and squeezing it tight. I took that as a silent apology for his behavior and smiled for the cameras as I slid out of the limousine behind him.

We waved. We laughed. We posed. The paparazzi asked questions. We answered them. One asked if we were engaged by the sizable rock on my finger. A question I was dreading as we were clearly not, and I would have never wanted to make the public think we were. But when I laughed and shook my head, Tommy went still. He reached for my left hand, raised it to his lips and kissed the ring. The crowd of cameras flashing went wild, blinding me with every click. I couldn't understand what just went down, but part of me felt like I had been used, and I didn't know why.

A knot formed in my stomach. My family was watching this from home. My friends. I felt tears forming when I thought of my parents thinking I'd gone off and gotten engaged without them even knowing about it. I couldn't let this happen. I couldn't let people think this was true. So, when the first person asked me for an interview, I said yes.

"Good evening, Sadie. You look absolutely-—wow. Breathtaking doesn't even begin to describe this western-chic look you're going for. So, tell me. Who are you wearing tonight?"

"Thank you so much. I'm wearing Los De La Blanc, a French Montana western brand, from head to toe. And the jewelry is from—," she cut me off.

"This is from that store on Rodeo Drive! *Gilded Spurs!*" Relief washed over me as she recognized it. Less explaining.

"Yes, that's the place. Of course, I was supposed to wear this ring on my *right* hand, but see, I jammed that finger, and..." I trailed off, realizing this was awkward now as Tommy waltzed over and put his arm around me. Suddenly, I felt like he was supervising the conversation.

"It looks stunning on you. Thank you, Sadie. Now, Tommy—this is quite a night for you! Out of the seven nominations, which one do you think is most likely 'in the bag'?"

"Honestly, I think I have a solid chance for any of them. But that 'Best Actor in Hollywood' award is really calling my name. I mean, if I could win that, it would just be solidifying things that people have been saying for years, right?" The woman interviewing Tommy ate it right up.

"Oh, *absolutely!* If you don't win that, who will? Let me see who else is in the category. Ha! It's the guy from that animated television show where he dresses up like the monkey. Oh, Tommy. You have that one in the bag!"

Tommy didn't take his arm off of me while he spoke, and I just stood there, smiling like it was my job, while the thoughts of people thinking we were engaged bothered me. I knew I was obsessing, and I said a prayer under my breath about it. But could I *really* see myself marrying Tommy? Sure, he was a dream to date. He took me out every weekend. He was the biggest hunk in all of Hollywood. A total dreamboat. But I was starting to wonder... Did I like him? Tonight, on two occasions, he'd already made me feel uncomfortable. On our supposed "debut" as a couple. While we'd been on several dates around

Los Angeles, photographed at restaurants or going to the movies and coffee, red carpet events were notoriously known for something people took their partners to. You didn't just take a fling on the red carpet. Not usually, anyway.

When we were finally free of the interviews, we shuffled into the large auditorium. An usher told us where to sit. There were cameras everywhere, filming every reaction people had. I was on my best behavior, afraid the camera might catch my touching the inside of my nostrils or making sure my bra was securely in place. For now, I'd just have to trust my glam team that I didn't have spinach in my teeth or a booger hanging from my nose. I said another silent prayer as the awards started to happen. I knew from the program, I was up for one in the first few minutes. *Best Supporting Actress in a Major Motion Picture.* It would be a huge honor to receive the award. If God wanted me to win it, I would. I already had my speech ready to go. And when it finally came time to announce the winner of my category, with Tommy's arm around me, squeezing me tightly in anticipation, I lost to Maddie Lane, for her role in *The Rhubarb Pie Pact,* a movie with a two-star rating. Clapping for her win, the cameras went off of Maddie and straight to me.

Tommy decided to take this moment to turn to me, take my face in his hands, and kiss me. We'd kissed each weekend, exactly once each time, as I told him already that I was abstaining from most things in the physical realm, but the public display of this was too much. I pulled my face back, to which he gripped in his hands harder. By the time I wriggled myself free, the cameras had moved back to Maddie, who gave her acceptance speech, thanking her managers and husband who owned the production company.

By the time Tommy's categories started getting called, I was still reeling from the kiss. It was too much. He'd never acted this way before. He'd always been sweet, kind, and gentle, agreeing with me that he wanted to take things slow and go at my pace. But something had changed in him tonight. Ever since I made that comment in the limousine about him not being a real cowboy… Did he take that to heart? Did that really *offend* him? I mean, it was nothing but the truth. Sure, I could have said it more tactfully, but I was teasing him. We both knew that he'd never done anything *cowboy* in his life.

"And the winner is… Tommy Wheeler!" As Tommy went up for his first, second, and third wins of the night, I stopped acting surprised. He downed a glass of champagne with each win and came back to his seat boozier than before. As the final award of the night came up, *Best Actor in Hollywood,* a title that itself was a little egotistical, I actually started to pray that he didn't win. As it was, he was acting like he could use a little humbling. Sure, I got my dose tonight, but all glory to God. It—that award—wasn't meant for me. All of these wins were just going to go to his head. How could they not?

"I shouldn't be surprised as I hold this envelope and see the winner's name," the stunning Puerto-Rican actress, Makayla Barnes, announced from the podium. Her glittering, white dress, that looked like she was about to get married, was flowing down like a wedding cake. Now *that* was a style I wished I was wearing tonight. I looked over at Tommy, feeling a little hurt that I wore what he asked me to. Heck, I agreed to it, willingly. But this was my first awards show, and I was nominated, and I wished I had worn what I wanted to wear. The only person I could blame was myself. As she called Tommy's name, as we all knew she would, Tommy stood up and punched the sky, his jet black cowboy hat falling off his head. People in the crowd started laughing, which threw off his balance.

As he reached down to pick up the hat, someone behind us hollered out, "Better get your hat, cowboy," and Tommy froze again. Was he piping mad or embarrassed? I really couldn't tell. But either way, I didn't like it. Either way, this night was soured from the moment I made that comment. Tommy's drinking and sweeping wins weren't earning any respect from me; in fact, the whole thing was turning me off. Where was the sweet, humble guy that I met a few weeks ago? Okay, maybe he'd never been humble, but the man I was with tonight was far from sweet. The camera came around to me one more time, as Tommy made his way up the stage. I'd removed the ring from my left hand, finding that it fit on my right pinky well enough that it wouldn't slip off. Heck, I wouldn't have wanted to cover the cost of this rock if it did. I was tempted to pull off my earrings, as they were weighing down my ears like doorknockers, but I left those on. The camera lingered. I gave a smile and a wave, clearly making the sacrifice that it was looking for as the camera moved back on to Tommy. Just in time for the cringiest acceptance speech in history.

Sweat was beaded on his dark, furled brow. He looked like he could barely stand up. "I want to thank... Myself. I won this award. I did it. Thank you, Tommy!" A far cry from the man who said his faith in God was the most important part of his life. *Lord, You've opened my eyes to something tonight. Thank You.*

CHAPTER 3

Sadie

After the award show, Tommy took a phone call from his agent who was screaming on the other line. It was all I could do to not listen in, but it was clear that he was livid about the egotistical speech, saying things like "This won't make us any new friends." If by *friends,* he meant connections, then yeah. No one wants to work with a diva, and Tommy just put himself in diva land.

The biggest blessing from that phone call? Tommy switched to drinking water. He sobered up. The buzz was officially killed. We went to our first after party at no other than Maddie Lane's sprawling Hollywood Hills estate.

"Champagne?" a waiter carrying a silver tray with diamond-cut champagne flutes filled to the brim asked me.

"No, thank you. I don't drink." I gave a smile.

"You don't have to explain yourself," Tommy grumbled. "They are working for us. They don't need to know that goody two-shoes here is too good for a drink." My eyes widened.

"Excuse me?" I asked, crossing my arms. This was turning downright bad. Tommy huffed, and puffed, and relented, putting his arm back around me.

"Look, I'm so sorry, Sadie. I royally screwed up with the champagne. This isn't me, and you know that." I knew that this wasn't him, but I also didn't deserve it, either. I had a sneaking suspicion this had everything to do with his agent's phone call.

"The speech wasn't great," I said, deciding to go for it.

"Kick me while I'm down." He put his hands in the air. I shrugged.

"I wasn't listening in, but look, the whole world could hear the screams of your agent tonight. I agree with him. The ego wasn't a good thing. How are you going to make up for it? What's the plan?" I was a woman of action and wanted to know what PR stunt he was going to pull to smooth this out. After all, everyone could get redemption. "Public apology?"

"You think I should apologize for my speech?" His jaw dropped. I shrugged and nodded.

"I mean, yeah. I do. It wasn't in good taste."

"Listen, Sadie. You're a little green around the gills in this industry, wouldn't you say?" His tone had deepened. At this point, I wasn't sure where this night was going to end, but I might have just needed to get a taxi home.

"I might be new in this glittering world, Tommy, but I know about staying humble. None of this is guaranteed. God can take it away any time." Tommy froze for a moment, pausing on my words about God.

"I'm not apologizing to anyone except you," he smiled, taking me in an embrace. I welcomed it, feeling like he was finally back to normal. Everyone could have had a bad night, and Tommy certainly had one. But my earlier question, if I even liked him, was not far from my mind. "I'll never touch champagne again. Clearly, I can't handle it. Cowboys don't mix with bubbles." I held back my laughter, choosing to also hold my tongue and not add in a snarky comment about him not being a real cowboy. Sometimes, you just had to let someone win.

*****

After ten minutes at a different after party, my designer boots were killing my feet, and I was feeling tired of hanging on Tommy's arm. Sure, I was enjoying being his girlfriend, but tonight just wasn't the vibe I was looking for. I took respite in a hanging wicker chair outside, that overlooked a gorgeous, glowing pool shaped like a lagoon. The area was landscaped to a hilt—glowing lights throughout full bushes, flowers that looked both overgrown and manicured, large, colorful rocks placed around everything. It was so peaceful out here, I took the time to thank God for this experience. But as people shuffled in and out of the mansion behind me, their laughter grew louder as the bottles were uncorked, and the glittering excitement of the night faded.

"I'm going to catch a cab back home," I told Tommy, as I found him in the center of the party, schmoozing everyone there. Tommy at first flashed me a look of betrayal, but then his eyes quickly softened. I noticed a champagne flute in his hand, not twenty minutes after he swore off of it. When he followed my gaze to the flute, he shook his head.

"Someone just handed this to me. I'm not drinking it, I promise." He set it down on the nearest surface and put his arm around me a little too tightly. "Well, the lady would like to go back home now," he announced loudly, with an implication of something else to his tone. Men in the room were smiling and nodding at us, while Tommy ate it up. Once again, I couldn't let it slide.

"Yeah, it's past my bedtime. I have church in the morning." The room went stiff and silent.

"You're such a mood killer," Tommy teased, whispering into my ear.

"How so?" I looked at him innocently. He shrugged and started his goodbyes as we made our way to the door.

Tommy's driver headed down the lane as we sat comfortably in the back of the limousine. I watched the mansions disappear behind the rolling hills and daydreamed of taking off my boots. The straps of my dress still stuck to me with their adhesive. *Maybe I should jump in the pool when I get home?* The dress was given to me; I didn't need to return it. Besides, I doubted I'd ever wear it again. I smirked at the thought.

"What's so funny?" Tommy pressed, his boozy breath on my neck.

"My dress is glued to me. I'm just wondering how I'm going to remove it without taking my skin off with it," I said with a laugh. Tommy's eyes traced down to my bodice.

"I'll help you with it," he said, grabbing my waist.

"Nice try, Tommy." I rolled my eyes and smiled. He went still.

"Why not?" he asked.

"Because, I told you. I'm not putting myself in a position where things can get out of hand. I made a commitment to save all things physical for marriage, remember?" I told Tommy that on our first date, when he asked if I wanted to come back to his place after dinner. He seemed genuinely fine about it at the time. Plus, given his Christian faith, I didn't think he was opposed to the same ideas. Until now, when he *rolled his eyes back at me.*

"C'mon, Sadie. Do you know how the world works?" He removed his hands from my waist and crossed his arms.

"In fact, I do." Knowing full well that this relationship had now run its course.

"I didn't think you were serious about that." His tone dropped, and his voice sounded softer. "I thought you were just playing hard to get."

"I'm as serious as the plague." I crossed my arms, not wanting his hands on me again. I looked back out the window and saw we were headed in the opposite direction of my house. I sprung forward, opening the privacy partition.

"How can I assist you, Sadie?" the driver spoke.

"I live in the opposite direction," I croaked out, suddenly feeling emotional at the nights turn of events. The driver nodded with wide eyes.

"No problem, Sadie. Tommy just told me to take you both to his place. But how about we drop him off and then I promise, I'll take you straight home." Relief flooded my veins, and I sat back down, but this time, off to the side.

"Thank you," I said, not looking at Tommy.

"Really?" Tommy asked, hitting a button near his seat that closed the partition again. "This is how we are going to end the night?"

"Yes. I'm tired, my feet hurt and… I don't think this is going to work out." The words stung as I said them. Just this morning, I was thanking God for sending me a dreamboat for a boyfriend, and now? I was ending things.

"Don't be like that, Sadie!" he pleaded to me with his eyes. His handsome face bore at me. "I'm sorry, okay? I respect your boundaries. In fact, I'm impressed. Most women jump at the chance… Anyway, really, don't do this. I think I'm falling in love with you." He leaned towards me and reached out his hand, covering the top of mine. My cheeks flushed. Here I was, in the back of a limousine with Hollywood's darling, and he was telling me that he was falling in love with me. What did I say to that? Despite tonight, I would have been lying if I had said I didn't feel the same way. Other than this trainwreck of an evening, he'd been nothing but doting, kind, and increasingly handsome every time I saw him.

"Thank you for saying that you respect my boundaries," I whispered, looking up at him. I could tell it wasn't exactly what he was looking to hear, but I didn't know what else to say.

"How about you walk me to my door?" he asked, as the limousine slowed to a stop. I looked outside, thinking the cooling air might feel good on my skin.

"Sure. And then, I'm going home," I said, to which he agreed and gave me a wink.

CHAPTER 4

Sadie

At Tommy's house, I stood at the edge of his landing, as far from the door as I could be. It was a modest estate—a modern home with large windows, dark gray siding, and a flat roof. When I first saw it, I thought it looked like a giant square. I still thought that.

"Back at the ranch," he said, leading me up the walkway. I scoffed, not daring to correct him, as I started to think, *Maybe this cowboy obsession is more of an identity crisis than anything.*

"Goodnight, Tommy," I said, ready to give him a warm hug and a peck. A nice, warm kiss had been how we ended our dates each weekend, and it was something I looked forward to greatly. Tonight, I was just ready to leave. But as I turned to go, he took my hand and pulled me in.

The sudden, frantic kiss felt desperate. He pulled me into him, holding me close with his hands on my back, and he tilted me backwards like we were doing some sort of elaborate dance. The flash of a camera in the distance let me know that we weren't alone out here. My hands went out to push him away, and the moment they made contact with his chest, he did just that, tilting me back upward. Once he removed his mouth from mine, we were both breathless.

"Goodnight, Sadie." And just like that, he walked into his big square home, wearing his cowboy getup, likely about to take a long bubble bath and go to sleep with reruns of his show on television.

I wasn't in love with Tommy Wheeler. In fact, I thought he was a creep. Tomorrow morning, before church, I'd call him and break up with him, respectfully.

*****

I awoke to my phone buzzing. Reaching for it, I knocked it off my nightstand onto the floor. My shoulders were still sticky with adhesive residue. Showering in the dress wasn't the greatest experience, but I was able to remove the straps without a trip to the emergency room, so I called that a win. My feet on the other hand? *I may be wearing flip flops until all of my blisters go away.* Those boots may have been beautiful, but pure treachery to walk in.

Instead of getting up to grab it, I let it continue to disturb my sleep for as long as I could stand it. I peeked out of my sleep mask. It wasn't even seven in the morning yet. What was so urgent on a Sunday?

Groaning, I got up and looked. I had forty-three new messages. Eleven from my manager, Janie. Four missed calls from her, too. One text from Molly.

Molly: He posted WHAT?

The sight of her words made me confused, but I needed to call Janie back.

"This better not be about the vampires," I said, as she answered on the first ring.

"What happened last night?" she demanded. A slew of terrible memories flashed into my mind.

"Are you talking about the awards show? Because I lost to Maddie–," she cut me off.

"I'm talking about what happened with Tommy."

"Absolutely *nothing* happened with Tommy. Why?" My sleep mask was now pulled up to my forehead, and my heart was picking up the pace. I didn't see myself getting any more sleep after this.

"It's over. He dumped you. And it's all over the tabloids that you were clingy, immature, and wanted too much for the poor bachelor, just looking to settle down." My eyes bugged out of my forehead as the color bled from my face.

"Excuse me?" I gasped for air. No matter what I did, I felt like I couldn't get enough oxygen.

"You're probably having a panic attack," Janie said, as a matter-of-factly, but with no sense of care in her voice. "Get it together. We have to fix this, or your career won't survive."

"I was... going to... break up with him!" I shouted in between gasps. "He's a jerk!" But no matter what I said, it didn't matter. I put the call on speaker and held my phone with shaky hands, opening my social media app. The photo that was snapped last night as Tommy kissed me as hard as he could was plastered everywhere. The headlines were terrible.

"Tommy's girl wanted too much from him"

"Clingy and desperate for attention"

"He's fighting her off as she holds on for dear life"

"I'm literally pushing him away in that kiss. Do you believe me?" I asked Janie, who had been rambling off about the PR needed to rectify the situation. She paused and took a breath.

"Yes, I believe you. But that doesn't matter, because in the court of public opinion, they are going to find Tommy innocent every time." I felt like tears were rolling down my face, but reaching up, my face was dry. I was having a panic attack, because my character was being lied about all over the internet.

"So, what do we do now?" I asked, as a tear eventually fell.

"We pray that this fire gets put out quickly and doesn't take your career with it." We hung up the phone, and I lay back on my pillow. *God, what happened? What spurred this? Didn't I do everything right?*

I remembered Janie's words about Tommy breaking up with me. I looked at my messages, none from him. I looked at my missed calls, none from him. My hands, still shaking, opened the social media app once more. I couldn't look at that photo again. It was the number one trending photo, and it made me ill. I clicked on Tommy's profile, where it alerted me that he had one new post. As I scrolled to see it, I couldn't believe my eyes.

A photo of him and me from last night on the red carpet. In this particular photo, with my too-dark of makeup and strained posture, I looked stressed. Unhappy. Like I was in need of a glass of prune juice. And yet, Tommy looked as handsome as I'd ever seen him. At first glance, I felt betrayed by him posting the worst photo of me that he could, but then I realized my vanity was getting the better of me. I didn't like that dress, that makeup; the entire getup wasn't me. This was only my fault. I scrolled down to the caption.

"Some people aren't who you think they are. Praying for clarity and loyalty for my next steps." If I hadn't already been horrified, I was now, as tears flooded my eyes to the point where I couldn't even see out of them. I tossed my phone, turning face-first into my down feather pillow.

"God, help me!" I cried out, giving the situation to Him. He knew my heart. He would get me through this.

*****

If I had to explain myself anymore today, I would go mute from the shock. While Janie was trying to handle most of the "fires," as she called them, I had been hearing from my family. My parents called, very concerned but respectfully wanting to know what was going on. The photo of Tommy and me kissing? Taken out of context, it was not great for my image. It was not great for my mental health. And having them see it was like someone pulling out the lynch pin that was holding everything in my life together until now.

"It's not what it looks like," I told my mom, who had me on speaker phone. "I promise you that. I was pushing him away," I said, as tears started to fall while I choked up.

"I believe you, sweetheart. Say, why don't you come home for a while? Regroup. Your cousin Sandy just got her new salon opened. We could go get pedicures." I cried again, agreeing that a trip home was just what I needed.

"Do you have everything under control there, Sadie?" my dad asked in the background. "I don't think I like you dating some hotshot that thinks he can have his hands all over you." I agreed with him.

"My manager is doing her best to fix this all. She says my career could really be in jeopardy over this, believe it or not." I closed my eyes, pinching the bridge of my nose. "But it's going to be okay. Whatever is the Lord's will for my life, I accept. Maybe I'm meant to be a school teacher after all," I teased, as though I'd always dreamed of being an actress. In my lanky, awkward high school years, my guidance counselor had told me

I would make a great school teacher. No one else thought so but her.

"Don't give up so easily, Sadie. Weather the storm. God is working through you right now despite all of this. The truth will prevail. This, too, will bear fruit." My mom always knew what to say.

"And you really missed your calling to become a motivational speaker, Mom." We made a few plans for me to fly out west to visit them for a few days and ended the call.

That night, as I packed my small suitcase, my phone rang. Today, each call was harder to take. Janie's name flashed, and I hesitantly answered it.

"Vampires backed out," she said hastily. I wasn't disappointed in the least, but I was concerned why they would be backing out from me.

"What do you mean, they backed out? Are they not filming anymore?" I asked.

"They don't want *you,* Sadie." The words stung.

"I didn't want that movie anyway. I told you that yesterday," I said, trying to regain some of my power in this powerless situation.

"That's not the point. If they are backing out—a movie that was destined to flop, only to be resurfaced ten years later and turned into a cult movie because it's ironic for kids then to watch lame flicks—then the rest is surely to follow. Actually, hold on." My face turned red. Everything was so out of control. I didn't ask for any of this. Why was Tommy treating me this way? He was bending everything into lies. He was a liar. "Okay, I'm back. The sharks are out, too. I'm sorry, Sadie. This is how the world works." My Australian movie shoot—gone. This time, I felt devastated.

"What was their reasoning? What did they say?" I was silently crying on the other end of the phone. I hated feeling this out of control.

"It's because they think it's right to side with Tommy. If he casts you aside, or at least, makes it look that way, they certainly don't want to be on your side, either."

"But he's a liar! He's lying about all of this. I wouldn't go home with him last night, and after that speech—good gracious. We got into an argument, and he blindsided me with this." Janie listened patiently as I rambled on.

"Would you like to make a statement to that effect? With what you just told me—that he's a lying, full of himself creep, whose cowboy persona has become downright delusional!?" Though it was a tempting offer, I'd already said too much. Thankfully, Janie had an NDA, which made her more like a therapist in that sense. I knew whatever I told her, it ended here.

"I don't want to stoop to his level." Janie let out a sigh.

"You're one of the good ones, kid. But I can't promise this isn't the end for you. I'm going to do what I can, because I really believe in you. I'll call back when I have something for you." And that was it. With that call, my calendar was cleared. I had no more work coming up. I had no offers. I wished that I had a landline so that I could at least check the dial tone.

The coming weeks would be as quiet as they ever were. Other than the call from the Gilded Spurr requesting their jewelry back, my phone stopped ringing. And just like that, my career was over.

*****

"Sadie Clark?" The real estate agent, Millie Marks, got out of her shiny white Lexus.

"Yes. Nice to meet you." We shook hands. Her long, red acrylic nails caught the glare of every light around. She had long, thick, brown hair and tan skin and was fit as a fiddle.

"I used to be an actress too," she said, as we took the elevator up to my third floor condo.

"Really?" I asked with wide eyes. I could certainly believe it. She was absolutely gorgeous.

"Yeah. I had a few roles in some direct-to-DVD movies." Her laugh was brilliant. "Then, I met my husband. He owns my real estate agency." She motioned to the beautiful briefcase she was carrying that had an emblem embroidered on it. "Turns out, there is life after acting. And the thrill of selling real estate is pretty amazing."

"Life after acting, huh?" It was like she was reading my mind. Despite my career going ice cold overnight, I still felt the Lord was telling me to wait. Hold steady. Subletting my apartment was part of that waiting.

"So, are you taking a big trip somewhere? Filming on location? I think I heard you are doing that shark movie in Australia. Pretty cool!" Millie came by it honestly, and I didn't get the feeling she was trying to pump me for information or anything like that. I gave her honesty in return.

"I'm going home for a while. I need a break from the glitz and the glamour of Hollywood," I said with a smile. "I lost out on that shark movie, unfortunately." Millie's eyes fell solemn.

"It happens, girl. Hollywood is a tough place to make it, that's for sure."

"That it is."

After we set the terms of my sublet agreement, I had a handful of days to move out. I was going to be gone for three months to start. Janie and I had just put out a new round of headshots. I updated my acting reels. We posted a video montage of my best scenes to date. If those didn't strum up any interest, I could extend my sublet or sell the place altogether.

Since I had gotten a great price for the condo, and I had bought it outright, the rent was actually pretty amazing. I was used to living on little income my whole life. This was more than enough to survive back home in Ohio. But the thought of returning made my stomach do a flip.

I loved my parents endlessly. God, family, and acting—those were my passions, in that order. But I wasn't ready to give up and make any permanent decisions. It was just that sitting here waiting was making me crazy. Every time I went outside, and I saw paparazzi stalking me for photos of the poor, lonely actress who got dumped by Tommy Wheeler, I felt worse. I wanted nothing more than to set the record straight. But how would that make me look? Tommy would deny it anyway. Say it was slander. Then where would I be?

Social media was even worse. Not only did Tommy delete all of our photos—except the breakup post, which he pinned to the top of his profile—but he'd been posting photos of him in one ridiculous cowboy getup after another, with captions like, "Single and ready to rope". Or, my personal favorite, "Focusing on faith and career." If anything, Tommy was spiritually sick. But regardless of his situation, I was praying that he found God and corrected his path.

On the last night in my condo, my bags were packed. Everything except my clothes and makeup was staying here. I had very few personal effects, and those all fit in my purse. A purple leather Bible, given to me by my parents when I was a teen. A promise ring that I bought myself when I made a commitment to keep my purity until I was married. A few Polaroids that I snapped when I first moved here, mostly of the palm trees, when this whole town felt romanticized.

The weather here was something else. I'd give it that— it felt like paradise. Not too hot. Not too cold. Just perfect. A cool, beachy breeze the closer you got to the beach. The feeling that anything was possible, under the endless sunshine. That was why people came here with big dreams. I couldn't say I wouldn't miss it. But in paradise, the sun still set. And for now, it was my time to leave. Pulling out my phone, I called Molly.

"Those darn birds!" Molly was shrieking, as loud chatter could be heard in the background.

"Molly? Are you okay?" I asked with hesitancy.

"Yes, sorry, Sadie. I put a birdfeeder outside of my house, and the birds decided my car was their toilet." I couldn't help but laugh at the visual. "They've been playing toilet target practice all morning! It's absolutely *covered,* Sadie." Instantly, I felt better. We chatted idly for a few minutes regarding the state of her car while she ran around, shooing the birds off of the feeder. "No more seed for you guys! Only hummingbird feeders from now on." I was in stitches, laughing, when the conversation came around to me.

"I'm subletting the condo," I said, wearily. She just responded with an "Uh-huh." "Just for a few months, probably."

"Okay."

"You're not going to ask why?"

"Do you want me to ask why?" I wrestled with the thought. "Because I already know you've prayed about it." She was right about that.

"I'm coming home for a while."

"Good. You can help me swat these birds away that now think they've found their new favorite rest stop."

"Good? That's it?" Part of me did want her to ask why. To try and plead with me. To talk me out of... anything.

"Sadie, this is home, not exile. You act like this is the biggest defeat you've ever faced. May I remind you of prom when we did our own makeup, and every photo we had ghostly white faces from that powder?" I shrugged with a smile.

"Well, it feels like failure."

"You paid off your parents' house at twenty-four. You didn't compromise your faith. You didn't go home with a man who tried to manipulate you. And you're worried about failure?"

"Everyone thinks I'm clingy. Desperate. I didn't even do anything."

"I know. But the people who actually matter know." She was right about that.

"I'm scared it's over," I admitted.

"Then let it be over for a minute. Let God work

through this storm for you. Give it to Him. Come home. Get a pedicure. It will be like old times. But through it all, let God work. Maybe there's some handsome hunk out here He wants you to meet instead."

"I'm not thinking about men," I said with a burst of air. That was the last thing I needed to be thinking about for a long, long time.

"That's a cute thought, but you realize, that's when they show up, right? Besides, you are not this situation, Sadie. Don't write off love just because someone wronged you."

"You're my best friend forever, you know that?"

CHAPTER 5

Sadie

I was already in the car heading for the airport when Janie called me. I hadn't heard from her in two weeks already, and in Hollywood, that's a long time for your phone not to ring.

"Good morning," I said, full of caffeine from my luxurious espresso machine and the Holy Spirit from the morning's devotion. I was in a good place. Janie's voice sounded perky as well.

"I got something for you, but I don't know if you'll want it." My eyebrow cocked. What sort of proposition was that?

"Okay. What is it?" My interest was piqued.

"Have you heard of the Christian Production Company?" I had not just heard of it; I'd watched several of their movies on the Christian movie channels I subscribed to.

"Of course I have. Do they want me in a role?" I asked, sounding a little too eager, sure. But whatever it was, Janie sounded like she wasn't convinced this was a good offer.

"Yeah, they do. There's a role for a cheesy western movie being filmed in Wyoming next month. Their lead actress broke her arm falling off a horse in an unrelated incident in Texas and now can't do the film, I guess. More of a fear of horses it sounded like." My eyes widened.

"Even with my scandal and all that, they want me?" I couldn't believe my luck in getting interest, especially after the kiss with Tommy going viral.

"Look, I don't know if I would consider this role at your level. In a way, these low-budget indie films are beneath you. But, maybe it's all that's left, for now. Who knows, though? Do a good job, maybe more will come from it." While I certainly didn't feel that any role was beneath me, I knew what she meant. I had gotten a lucky break by being cast in a major summer blockbuster film off of a headshot and a short screen test. To be honest, I'd never really felt like I paid my dues to start with. Though now, with Tommy, I had certainly been through enough of a ringer to never want to act again. I could feel the Lord nudging me that this was not time to give up.

"I'll do it," I said, without even thinking about it.

"Don't say yes out of desperation, Sadie. It could be that more will come."

"I'm not desperate. I am interested in filming for the network, and I'd like to be associated with Christian films. It's good for my brand." I could hear Jamie scoff under her breath, clearly not in agreement with me.

"Whatever you say. But good. I'll set it up." She was typing on her computer in the background. "You'll need to be in Dust Creek, Wyoming, next week."

"Dust what?" I'd never heard of the place in my life.

"Dust Creek. There's even an airport there. You'll be filming on a real dude ranch, and someone will be by to pick you up. I'll send you all the nitty gritty details over shortly. Are you home? A courier could be by in an hour," she asked, tapping her nails on her desk, waiting for my answer.

"I'm actually on my way to the airport. I just sublet my condo for three months." The words coming out of my mouth made me feel like I had jumped the gun, but Janie didn't miss a beat.

"That's fine. Give me the address of where you're going, and I'll have it faxed over and delivered to you."

"Thank you for finding me this deal, Janie." I meant it.

"You're welcome, Sadie. I may have put your headshot in front of a few people that I happen to know who think Tommy Wheeler is a complete tool," she confided. I almost felt tears coming on from praise. God was faithful. I was getting another chance. I'd be filming a Christian movie. What more could I have wanted?

That night, as I arrived at my parents' newly paid-off bungalow that backed up to a forest of stunning oak trees, a courier was parked outside.

"Ms. Clark?" he asked, holding a manilla envelope.

"That's me," I said. He handed me the envelope with a nod.

"It's nice to meet you. You are just as pretty in person, you know." His face reddened, and I felt mine blush in surprise.

"Thank you so much," I said, lingering for a moment, unsure if I should walk away or not. He was about my age, but the last thing I needed right now was to be entertaining the idea of any man. I was trying to get my career back off of its derailment.

Before I could say or do anything else, the courier got back in his car and sped off. "Alright, then," I said, letting out a laugh under my breath.

Seeing my parents again felt great. I may have only been here a few weeks ago, but that was a hopeless time where we pretended I wasn't in hiding. Pretended not to see my name splashed over all the headlines. Tommy was the talk of the country, basking in his win of "Best Actor in Hollywood," and there I was, cast aside by the same industry off of a perceived event that didn't even happen.

Now, walking into their home, I had better news.

"The Christian Production Company!?" They both beamed at the announcement, while I held the script and contract in my hands, still unopened.

"That's right. Well, I better go figure out what my role will be." I headed straight for my old room, kicked off my shoes, and drew a bath in the ensuite. After I put on a white, fluffy robe and pulled my hair back, I sat on the edge of the tub while the water filled the basin and opened the envelope.

The Belle of Bitter Creek directed by Rufus McAdams

Tagline: "When her reputation is ruined, only truth can set her free."

Synopsis: In 1887 Wyoming Territory, a celebrated frontier performer is falsely accused of scandal and cast out of high society. Forced to seek refuge at a struggling cattle ranch, she must rebuild her life the hard way—discovering that identity rooted in applause will always crumble, but identity rooted in faith will stand.

I put the script down, stunned. This all sounded a little familiar, didn't it? "God, you sure do have a sense of humor." I turned off the water to the tub, climbed in, picked the script back up off the tub's ledge, and dove into the story.

That night, after a very refreshing script read and a long bubble bath, I texted Molly to tell her the news.

Sadie: Change of plans.

Molly: You're not shaving your head are you?

Sadie: No.

Molly: Okay, good. Continue.

Sadie: I just accepted a role.

Molly: Wow! See? The Lord is working! From where?

Sadie: The Christian Production Company.

Molly:...Are we being punked?

Sadie: It's a western.

Molly: Of course it is.

Sadie: Filming in Wyoming. On an actual ranch.

Molly: You're telling me that the man who publicly humiliated you is a fake cowboy... and now God is sending you to real cowboys?

Sadie: When you say it like that, it sounds dramatic.

Molly: It *is* dramatic. This is God-level irony.

Sadie: I leave tomorrow. So, I won't get to see you, and I'm sorry about that.

Molly: Okay, but listen carefully. If a rugged ranch hand with emotional stability and no social media presence appears...

Sadie: Molly.

Molly: ... I expect detailed reports.

Sadie: I'm going there to work.

Molly: You are going there to heal. Working is just a side quest.

CHAPTER 6

Sadie

The small airport looked more like an outbuilding than a terminal as the plane taxied over to it. The day had been long—after flying into Denver, a long, drawn-out layover in the basement of the airport where I then had to walk outside and climb a set of stairs onto the smallest commercial plane I'd been in. It was like flying private, except it was a small, single seat row airplane that just served coffee and peanuts.

"Welcome to Dust Creek, Wyoming," the captain said on the intercom. "If this is your last stop, we hope you enjoy your stay." Peering out the window as the plane came to a halt, the tall mountains that surrounded the airport still had a fresh pack of snow at the tops. *Where would one go from here, if this wasn't the destination?* I asked myself. I highly doubted this airport had any connecting flights. I'd bet on this being it, for the day, in fact.

Stepping off the plane, the air felt dry. A warm breeze was blowing through my hair. The line of people in front of me stopped while someone fumbled with the door. I closed my eyes while I waited, thanking God for making it safely, and the fact that there seemed to be little to no humidity here. Small wins.

As everyone crowded around the luggage carousel, most of the room was looking at me. Something that I had been used to these days. But I couldn't tell if it was because they recognized me or if it was just that small of a town, and they had never seen me before. It didn't matter either way, I supposed. All glory to God for whatever recognizability I had, as it meant I was living my dream of being in movies.

My luggage was last on the carousel. That always seemed to happen to me, but despite the room clearing out by the time it came, three young men came out of the woodwork offering to retrieve it for me.

"Thank you," I said to the young men who were standing there. They started arguing and pushing each other, duking it out among themselves who would get to pick it up for me. Before I could get concerned that my suitcase was going to roll back inside of the wall, an older man standing behind them picked up the handle.

"Sadie?" he asked, his eyes warm with a smile.

"Yes," I nodded. I knew someone from the ranch was coming to pick me up, but they never told me who.

"Billy Reed. From the Broken Arrow Ranch." He held out his hand to shake mine. The three young men left, but not without razzing each other even more. One yanked off another's cowboy hat and threw it. "Don't mind these kids. It's not every day we get a movie star in Dust Creek." I laughed and shrugged.

"I didn't know if anyone would even recognize me out here. Besides, I've just done that one movie. I don't know if that qualifies me as a movie star." I put my hand to my forehead, suddenly feeling a little dizzy.

"Here, I brought you some water," he said, leading me outside. "It's very dry here, if you haven't noticed. But if that don't get ya, the elevation will." He set my suitcase inside the truck bed and reached inside the truck, grabbing a bottle of water.

"Thank you," I said, cracking it open and taking a sip.

"You'll want to drink as much water as you can out here," he stalled.

"You sound like my dad," I laughed, taking another drink.

"I've got kids of my own, so that's probably why. Is this it for your luggage?" He pointed to my suitcase. "Travelin' pretty light for Hollywood, I'd say."

"Yeah. I left the stilettos, sequins, and glitter back home," I shrugged. Truthfully, there wasn't much I thought I should have brought. In my contract, I had daily laundry service and a concierge if there was anything I needed to have brought to me, so I just packed a few pairs of jeans, shirts, and some sandals that I was wearing. The rest of my suitcase was filled with toiletries, my hairbrush, and my Bible.

Once we were on the road, I noticed the cross necklace hanging from the rear-view mirror.

"This is pretty." I motioned to it. He nodded.

"It is. This is my son's truck. He's got mine attached to a thirty-foot trailer back at the ranch at the moment. He was supposed to come pick you up, but something came up last minute." I was intrigued hearing about the workings of the ranch, but I wasn't blind to the fact that Billy, a handsome man in his later years, had a son. My interest was piqued.

"Tell me about the ranch," I said, hoping that this would get Billy's gears going. I needed to learn everything I could about Wyoming to better play my role.

"We mostly raise horses," he started out, rubbing his chin. "We've got everything from Paints to Palominos. A few quarter horses, too. Had a Clydesdale once. I just loved his furry feet." He may as well have been speaking another language. I pulled out my phone to look up the type of horse.

"How do you spell that?" I asked, opening a web browser on my phone, before seeing that I had zero cell phone service. "Oh. We must be in a dead zone," I said with a sigh, putting the phone back in my pocket.

"I'm afraid not much is out here for cell service. Them phone companies are always wantin' to put up an ugly hundred-foot cell tower, but the residents don't want it. This is the downside. But don't you worry; we got that wireless internet back at the ranch. And I'll give you a show and tell of all the horse breeds myself. Better than Gargle." I let out a laugh.

"You mean, Google?"

"Whatever it's called. I don't know a thing about the internet. And that's a fact that I'm quite proud of."

We turned onto a country road that was full of potholes, and rode that for quite some time. It winded into a canyon of beautiful mountains, and we were surrounded by farms with cattle, horses, and sheep. As we drove, Billy took the opportunity to tell me about all the different kinds of animals, including the horse breeds, like he said he would. After hitting a sizable pothole, I bounced and hit my head on the roof of the truck cab.

"Sorry about that." He slowed down. "We had some recent rains that washed all of the sand out from the holes. It's time I go fill 'em again." I gave him a wide-eyed look.

"You have to take care of the roads?" He nodded.

"We all do. It's a town effort. There isn't much of a budget for roads and bridges out here since we voted for the fuel tax to be rerouted to the kids' school lunches." There was so much I didn't know about life—taxes were definitely one of them. I just nodded in reply.

"That sounds like an admirable effort." He shrugged at my words.

"We gotta take care of our kids. The thought of a child going without a meal, because their ranchin' family can't afford it, just don't sit well with us out here. Heck, most of these ranches are barely scrapin' by as it is." Looking around at the stunning landscape, that really surprised me.

"What about tourism? I certainly have never seen a place as beautiful as this!" He shook his head.

"We just got that one flight a day. Now, I ain't saying that tourists don't come here, because you look out at the reservoir on the 4th of July, and you'd be sayin' I was crazy to think this way. But the harder a place is to get to, the less it's traveled." He was right about that. Just me getting here from Ohio today was exhausting.

"It sounds like you have a bustling movie industry, at least." I grinned ear to ear, and Billy laughed, nodding his head.

"This was quite the blessing when we got the call from the Christian Production Company, that's for sure."

"How did they find out about the ranch? Or, is it your ranch?" I realized I didn't know Billy's role in the place.

"Yes. The ranch is in my family. My grandfather started it back in the late 1800's. About the time of the movie being filmed here, actually, so we dug out some of the ole' artifacts for the actors and actresses to use. But they found out about it on the internet. Of course, with my little knowledge of that topic, I have no clue on the workings or what. But I got a son in Denver, and he put it up on the internet somewhere. It's searchable, I do know that. He had some fancy cameraman come out and take photos. We get our fair share of foot traffic out this way. The Lord has blessed us."

We turned onto a dirt road, driving under a log archway that had a large sign depicting a broken arrow. The namesake of the ranch.

"How did the ranch get its name?" I asked. Billy grinned.

"My grandfather started this ranch. His wife was from the Shoshone tribe, and let's just say, her father was not happy about the marriage. He wanted her to marry the Chief's son. There was much anguish at the time for these star-crossed lovebirds. They married and started a small homestead on this land. With their skills put together, all of this was paid for by fur trapping in one winter. When her father saw her again the next spring, he saw that his daughter was happy. They already had a baby on the way. She had been brought to the Lord and shared her faith with him. And before he left their homestead, to head back to his camp in the Green River range, he broke an arrow over his leg, signifying that there was no war between the two of them. He accepted the marriage. At least, that's how I remember the story being told."

"Sounds like it would make a great movie!" I exclaimed. Billy, ripe with laughter, agreed.

"We will have to pitch it to the Christian Production Company."

After driving down the dirt road for what felt like forever, we dropped down over a hillside, and the ranch unfolded before my eyes.

A sprawling landscape peppered with towering pine trees, colorful horses, and beautiful log buildings was nestled against a mountain range. Below the mountains looked to be a roaring river. Billy parked the truck, and I couldn't wait to get out. The moment my feet touched the gravel, I felt like I had been transported to another world. Another time. Life out here was different of course. But I'd never experienced a peace like I had now, before I even walked around. Before I had spoken to anyone else. I felt like I was coming home for the first time. My home on earth, this side of heaven.

"Home, sweet home, for a few weeks!" Billy exclaimed, pulling my luggage out of the pickup bed. "We have you over here in this cabin. I'll walk you to it." He pointed to a beautiful log cabin that was sided with wavy, wooden shakes that looked like the branches of the ponderosa pine trees that surrounded it. I ran to the cabin, unable to hold back my excitement.

"It's perfect!" I shouted, meeting Billy's eyes with joy.

"Well, it ain't the Ritz, but I hope it will suit you." He opened the door, revealing a perfectly quaint living situation. A light wood kitchen with handmade cabinets that had as much charm as the outside. An orange tea kettle on the stove. A small dining room table with seating for two, topped with a brightly colored floral tablecloth, by the window. A cross hanging on the wall.

The bedroom had one bed, a little larger than a twin. It was dressed in bright, crisp white linens with an ample amount of down feather pillows. The kind of inviting bed that made you want to jump on it, face first into the pillows. The window looked out at the river, and without it even being open, I could hear the water rushing by. This was what peace looked like. This was what it felt like.

I decided to snap a few pictures to send to Molly. I knew she had been waiting for me to check in. After stepping outside, I held up my phone and took one of the sights and hit send, not bothering to look at it too closely. It had gorgeous mountains, some animals and people walking in the distance. She replied immediately.

> **Molly:** That's fake. That's a screensaver.
> **Molly:** Wait. Is that a cowboy in the background?
> **Molly:** Zoom. Enhance. Rotate.

I replied to her with some laughing emojis and the promise I would get back to her soon if anything fun happened. But before I could put my phone away, she sent another message.

> **Molly:** Is that a raccoon?

I looked up from my phone at the scenery I just photographed and sure enough, a raccoon was seen skittering off in the distance. I shrugged, chocking it up to the wilderness.

Billy had long left when I made it back to the front porch of my cabin, taking in every square inch of my temporary living arrangement. A pair of Adirondack chairs were positioned pointing the river. I knew this was where I would be having my morning coffee.

A low whistle brought me out of my daydream. All of the workings of the ranch were in motion, but I was supposed to be checking in with the director in a few minutes. Billy forgot to tell me where the clubhouse was, so now, I ventured off into the vastness of the ranch, following the sound of only a whistle.

A tall, broad-shouldered man stood with his back to me, whistling at his horses as they ran around an arena. *He must be signaling them for something,* I thought, *because they are not alerted to nor slowing at his whistle. Maybe it means for them to keep going?* Either way, as my feet crunched up behind him, I couldn't believe he didn't hear me. I needed to ask him for directions.

"Excuse me," I said, and to my surprise, he still didn't turn around. "Excuse me?" I spoke a little louder. He whistled again. I waited.

"I heard you," his deep, masculine voice that sounded like smooth leather and whiskey ran through my veins. "I heard you walking up a mile away. You can't sneak up on nobody in shoes like that." I looked down at my clunky sandals. His back was still to me.

"Can you tell me where the clubhouse is?" He held out an arm that pointed straight ahead from where I stood. "Thank you." I hesitated for another moment, curious to see if he was going to turn and face me, but to my disappointment, he didn't. I chugged on, walking another few hundred yards and into the clubhouse that was clearly marked so. Before going inside, I tapped out a quick message to Molly.

Me: There is a cowboy here who looks like he chops wood recreationally.

Molly: Giddy up, gorgeous!

Inside, a group of movie executives sat around in director chairs holding scripts. It was the exact cliche that everyone pictured when they imagined "filming on location." I was so thankful to God to be here—seeing this made me overjoyed with excitement.

"Sadie Clark." A man stood from his chair, setting his script down on the seat as I walked in the room. The rest of the group followed his lead as he shook my hand. "We are so happy to have you here as a part of this movie."

"I am happy to be here. Thank you all. This location is just stunning. I may never want to leave." My words surprised me when I said them. I'd never felt a connection to a place like I had here, and I'd been here less than thirty minutes.

"Well, I'm glad to hear it. I'm Rufus, the director. This is Mark. And Jesse. Tonya, and Kip." I shook all of their hands, both men and women who I had no idea what their roles were, other than Rufus, but I was excited, nonetheless.

"Nice to meet all of you." I let out a wave as I spoke. Everyone sat back in their chairs except Tonya.

"I'd like to review the filming schedule with you, if now is a good time?" she asked. I nodded.

"Sure." She walked us over to a table out in the center of the clubhouse.

"As you've become familiar with the story, you can see there's quite a lot of horses in this movie. Have you ever ridden before?"

"No, I haven't." Horses were not exactly the first mode of transport when you lived in Los Angeles.

"Okay, no worries. We have someone out here at the ranch that is going to familiarize you with horses and get you riding well enough that it feels authentic. It shouldn't take more than a few days. We can do it in between filming, as we are set to start tomorrow, and your horse scenes can all be filmed when we're up to speed." She grinned, giving me a false sense of confidence with the matter.

"That sounds good. How hard could it be?" Her laughter filled the room.

"You'll be fine, I hope!" She busted up laughing again, the brights of her eyes catching the light.

When Tonya and I were done, Mark introduced me to the ranch manager.

"Sadie, this is Pat." A woman in her sixties wearing denim jeans, a button up blouse tucked in, and a brown leather vest with a silk scarf tied around her neck greeted me.

"Nice to meet you, Pat." I reached out my hand and shook hers. She had kind blue eyes and long, grayish blonde hair pulled back in a loose braid that ran down her spine.

"You've already met Billy, I hear? He's my husband."

"Oh, yes! He picked me up from the airport."

"Wonderful. My role in this whole production is to organize the terms of your contract. Such as your daily laundry, ensuring you have the meals you want, and of course, sending someone into town to fetch what you need."

"Thank you so much, Pat. I should be good with what I have brought, but I will take you up on the others." As she gave me the rundown on where to leave my laundry each day on my cabin porch, we were facing the front windows. She pulled out a slip of paper from her vest, which outlined a daily breakfast, lunch, and dinner menu.

"Here is a sampling of some of the food that we serve here on the ranch. I'd like to get an idea right off the bat what you like, don't like, and any preferences you may have." I looked at the menu that she handed me. On the top was breakfast. Huevos Ranchos. Eggs Benedict. Ricotta pancakes. Lunch had everything from cold pasta salads to sandwiches. The back side had dinner, consisting of every type of steak, cooked any way, or fish.

"Oh my," I said, handing it back to her. "I may not fit into my wardrobe when I'm done here." I laughed, agreeing that the menu looked fantastic for my needs.

"That's great, Sadie. We just want to make sure you have everything you need here. My son, Rhett—," she trailed off as she looked up at the window. "Oh, there he is! He can get you whatever else you need." The broad-shouldered man from the horse corral walked by. I knew him by his clothes, his height, and his shoulders that looked like he could hold the weight of the world on them. But now, seeing his face took my breath away.

When he turned, I had to blink. Sun-tanned skin. Dark brows. A jaw covered in stubble that suggested he could grow a lumberjack beard in a few days. Dirt clung to him like it had no place it would rather be. The hat he wore was weathered, worn. He was a real, authentic, *cowboy.* He wasn't movie-star handsome. He was the kind of handsome that didn't know it or didn't care. Unfortunately for me, was worse. Pat cleared her throat, pulling me out of my one-man staring contest.

"Rhett will be teaching you how to ride horses." She nudged me with her elbow, clearly aware of the effect her son was having on me. "You know, he's about your age. He's 26. I always hoped he'd settle down and get married. He just needs to find the right woman." I turned to her, my cheeks roasting. *Was his mother telling me she wanted us to get married? She couldn't be. That would be crazy. We haven't even formally met.* But by the looks of that man, I was starting to feel as obsessed with cowboy culture as Tommy Wheeler.

CHAPTER 7

Rhett

The woman has been here all of five minutes, and already my day had been turned upside down.

I knew she was pretty. That came with the territory of Hollywood actresses. I even had watched her in that poker movie last summer. But seeing her in person, in blue jeans, casual footwear that wouldn't last five minutes in the wild, and without a stitch of makeup on? I wasn't prepared for that. Her beauty didn't come from her fancy hair, clothes, or drowning in the glamour of the bright lights of California. It came from within. She was as beautiful inside as she was out, and that was clear from the one glance I took her way when my dad brought her home from the airport.

My afternoon tradition in the warm months was to walk the perimeter of the cabin and look for rattle snakes. They were bad for business, no doubt, and even worse for Hollywood people. You got a normal person witnessing one slithering around, sure, they were going to yelp out. Maybe even hole up in their cabin until I could come out there and take care of it. But did any of these actors or actresses see one? Whose careers and livelihoods were built on the dramatics? Why, if they didn't call 911 after seeing one, setting off a five-alarm fire, and having the coast guard arrive by helicopter to airlift them out, I'd be surprised. Nah, the snakes weren't too good for business. Especially not for these folks.

There I was, about done with my perimeter check, when I heard my pops pull up in his pickup truck. I was ready to do a meet and greet with this girl, sure. I wasn't afraid of a Hollywood beauty. But then, as I turned a corner of a cabin not one hundred yards away, I stopped in my tracks like I had just found a nest of rattlers. She was far more beautiful than I ever imagined. She was enigmatic. Her laughter spoke the language of my heart. Her mannerisms showed she was gentle, honest, and excited. She put her hand to her chest when she saw the cabin. As she leapt for joy at her surroundings, I was nearly brought to my knees. If this weren't love at first sight, I didn't know what was.

I didn't know the mysteries of the Lord, and I wasn't trying to say I did. But what kind of game could God have been playing, when the first woman I felt this way about was one of these Hollywood people? I wasn't about that life. There wasn't one part of my soul that could have ever left Wyoming and lived under those fancy palm trees and flashing lights of the cameras. I couldn't have lived performatively. I couldn't have been on broadcast every move I made.

This poor woman had every choice she'd ever made splashed across the headlines. Though, half that stuff wasn't even real. I certainly didn't believe everything I read. Maybe she would tell me what happened. Maybe she wouldn't. *Rhett, get a grip!* I couldn't believe I was already hoping we'd have deep conversations where she shared her private life with me. I didn't know this woman, and the only thing I did know right now was I needed to pray.

God, please protect my heart. My mom had been beating the war drum of me getting married and settling down for years. Even my dad, sweet Billy, had encouraged me to find a nice wife. If it had been that easy, sure, I may have entertained the idea. But living out here, in the middle of nowhere Dust Creek, Wyoming- population 2500, most of which appeared to be twice my age, half my age, or already married off the moment they turned eighteen—the odds had never been in my favor.

There were quite a few bars in town, but I didn't drink. And I didn't like to witness the shenanigans of those drunk around me. Our local church wasn't much help, as most of the attendees were older. Like, older than my parents. Once, they tried to host a "Singles" event that ended disastrously. If it hadn't been directly after a service, I wouldn't have been able to walk by the room as I was heading for my truck. There were a handful of teens and some elderly widows who were already getting paired off in the time it took me to walk the five steps. That was fast.

The only woman in town that had ever interested me even the slightest bit was Sophia Banks. Sure, she was cute, but quiet. Like me. She was pretty, I thought. The problem was, so did my little brother, Wyatt.

I remember it like it was yesterday. Wyatt, around sixteen at the time, came home from a youth group retreat. "I found the one," he announced to my family, as he walked in the door, a heavy backpack strap slung over one shoulder. My parents both gave him a wide-eyed look that turned into laughter.

"So, you had a good time then, son?" my dad asked.

"She's the one. I just know it. I'm going to marry her." He dropped the backpack, the layer of dust and dirt covering it shaking off onto the wood floors of our log home.

"Why don't you go take a shower and then we can hear all about her?" my dad suggested. I, too, was interested in hearing about her. I was almost eighteen, two years older than Wyatt, and had yet to date. It was just us two kids, and I never felt like either one of us were in a rush to date or marry, though women had certainly been aware of us, and us of them. We were known around town as the Reed Romeo's, and though I didn't understand the nickname at the time because I certainly wasn't out flirtin' my way through the town prairie, a lot of the girls had crushes on us. Including Sophia Banks.

After Wyatt got himself cleaned up, he came back into the living room, standing a little straighter. His hair was gelled off to the side like I'd never seen it before. He was wearing a shirt with a collar, tucked into his jeans.

"Well don't you look nice?" my mother acknowledged, knowing full well her love-sick son was about to propose something to the room, hence, his clean appearance. My mother always was a sucker for a tucked in shirt.

"I'd like to have Sophia Banks over for dinner to meet everyone." My heart dropped into my stomach. There was no way that my little brother was pining for Sophia. Sure, I'd never even considered so much as saying hello to her. But I was waiting for God to lead my path in love.

"I think that will be swell," my mom agreed. "How about I call her parents?"

They married two years later, a week after graduating high school. Over the years of their marriage, I realized that I was never really drawn to Sophia like my brother was. He knew she was the one with a certainty reserved for those wise beyond their years. I had never been certain about anyone. I had never considered a second glance at anyone. Sophia was just quiet, with a mysterious quality about her that made me wonder if she could unfold before me into a woman that I might like to get to know.

Now, I knew for certain, that she would not have been the right kind of woman for me. They moved to Denver after marrying, both of them preferring a city life to the country landscape. Something I couldn't, and wouldn't, do.

Wyatt was always different from me. He might have been a ranch boy, through and through, but there was always more than this out there for him. He was always a little too eager to get away from here. On our pack trips through the mountains growing up, Wyatt always wanted to know what was over the next mountain. The next range. Just a little further, we could see if people were out there.

For me? I never wanted to see more people. More towns. I wanted more of this quiet, this peacefulness, this experiencing the presence of God in the stillness of the mountains. It didn't surprise me one bit that Wyatt and Sophia moved away shortly after marrying. In fact, I was happy for them. For my brother to get what he always wanted: people. Movement. City lights, traffic, and noise.

Now, years had passed. I'd just turned twenty-six, and I'd considered more than once that it might not have been the Lord's will that I marry. After all, other than a casual, misplaced intrigue in the woman that was meant for my brother, that ever since that day Wyatt had announced she was the one, I never had thought about for even a second that way again; I had never felt interest in anyone.

We had gotten our fair share of tourists out here at the Broken Arrow. We hosted weddings with ample bridesmaids and singles. We had even had a women's church retreat here once. But aside from a few shared glances, I'd never felt drawn to anyone. That was, until today.

Maybe it was her "star power." Was I starstruck? No, I didn't think so, because I had met a few of the other actors already and didn't react this way at all. Could it just be plain physical attraction? She was stunning, but it was so much more than that. I reflected in my heart. *Lord, I feel like I'm being pulled by a rope into her orbit, and my boots don't have enough traction to stop in the dirt. The ground is too dry, and the soles of my worn boots don't stand a chance.* For now, I decided it was best to keep my distance and see what God led me to do. I just didn't know if it was going to be that easy, considering I was giving her a riding lesson in an hour.

CHAPTER 8

Sadie

Pat invited me back to the lodge, where the dining room was scattered with perfectly circular wooden tables and log chairs. A votive and fresh cut hydrangeas were on every table. The scent was intoxicating: fresh air, floral, and sage from the bushes outside that were sprinkled all throughout the landscape.

The ceiling had to have been twenty feet or higher. A river rock fireplace ran all the way to the roof line. An oil painting of a woman with a hunting rifle hung above the helm. A young man was loading the fireplace with perfectly round logs.

"Sit wherever you like," she nudged, and after another moment of taking in the beauty of the room, I did just that, choosing a high-top table that overlooked the fireplace and had a view of the mountains through the large windows.

"I just can't get over this place," I said, as she brought me a sandwich the size of a basketball with a side of pasta salad and a big pitcher of lemonade, clinking as she walked from the ice.

"I hope you are hungry," she said, setting the plate down. It was enough food to last me for several lunches, normally, but when I saw it, my stomach rumbled like I hadn't eaten in weeks.

"Suddenly, I'm starving," I said, tearing into the sandwich. She nodded.

"It's the elevation. It makes you hungrier." She lingered while I bit into the delightful meal: roast beef, pickled red onions, salted tomato, and a thick aioli spread that was to die for.

"This is fantastic," I said between bites, taking a sip of the not-too-sweet lemonade that had a hint of something else. Pat read my expression like a book.

"I add lavender to my lemonade. It grows around here like weeds. Might as well use it," she winked, pulling out a chair next to me. "Do you mind if I sit?" I shook my head, drinking more lemonade.

"Not at all. I'd love the company." She smiled and nodded knowingly.

"You're not like the rest of them, you know."

"What do you mean?" I asked.

"The rest of the Hollywood people. You are so... down to earth. Humble. Kind."

"I never really understood the correlation of acting in movies and turning into a jerk." I shrugged my shoulders. "Besides, I have a keen understanding of what it feels like to have your phone stop ringing. The Lord gives; the Lord takes away. When this is all over, I'd like to know I never once stooped to the level of what this industry can do to people." Pat nodded like she knew exactly what I was talking about.

"So, some script, huh?" And that's when my suspicions were confirmed. She knew *exactly* what I was talking about. I looked out the window at the vast mountains. I felt safe with Pat. I was usually a great judge of character, except with Tommy, of course. Good looks could sometimes get in the way of reality for me, it seemed. I needed to be careful about that next time.

"When life imitates art," I said, turning back to her. We both laughed and she poured me another glass of her lavender lemonade.

After I ate as much as I could, Pat said she'd wrap the rest of it up for me and send it to my fridge. "In case you get snack-ish later," she winked. "Gotta put some meat on those bones of yours. You're a woman from the late 1800s, after all." We both chuckled at her comment.

"I suppose it wouldn't hurt if I put a little muscle on to look more realistic." I flexed my arms, revealing not much muscle in sight. We laughed some more. It was so easy talking to Pat. She felt like a friend right off the bat.

"You know what can help with that?" she asked, well after the laughter died down.

"What?"

"Horseback riding," she winked. "Rhett is set up to start you riding today." She looked at her watch. "In about an hour, actually." Suddenly, the food in my stomach felt like a brick as my nerves took hold.

"In an hour?" I felt a rush of panic wash over me, despite every cell in my body trying to tell me to relax. He was just a regular guy. A real, warm-blooded cowboy who looked like he could lift a refrigerator straight over his head kind of man.

"I must have forgotten to mention that Rufus thought you should start right away. You know, since it could take several lessons. Dozens, perhaps." Thinking of spending all that time with Rhett was intimidating. *Take a deep breath, Sadie. You don't know him.* As Pat cleared my plate, I tried to Jedi-mind-trick myself into ending this nervousness I had for a handsome stranger I had seen for fifteen seconds through a window. He might have had a high-pitched voice that sounded like he was plugging his nose. Except that didn't work, because his voice sounded like it bellowed from the pits of the earth. Deep. Masculine. Soothing.

What if he smelled like he'd been rolling around in a pig pen? Yes, that was it. He reeked. My mind went to the dirt that he was covered in. If I was dirt, I'd cling to him, too. *No! Not working!* Something about his appearance told me he smelled like a clean bar of soap and musk, despite his working hard all day. Men were just lucky like that.

Think, Sadie, think! What could repel me enough to get through this day while keeping him at a distance? I didn't need anything interfering with my role or my reputation. The world already thought I was desperate and clingy for Tommy, who was nothing but a *pretend* cowboy. This guy—he was the real deal, and I was ashamed to be feeling so attracted to him already. I was drawn to him like a fly on a horse's rear end. Then, it came to me.

Maybe he had such terrible breath from eating onions like apples all day. Perhaps he added a squeeze of roasted garlic on top before biting in. Yes. Just pretending he had the most extreme death-breath imaginable did lessen the attraction enough that I thought I could get through a horseback riding lesson with him and keep my dignity intact, focus sharp, and eyes on the Lord.

*****

Walking up to the horse corral, in a pair of boots that Pat left me in my cabin, I was aware of every bone in my body. I couldn't shake the stiffness out. I couldn't alleviate my nerves. As I walked up, he had his back to me, like before. But this time, I knew what he looked like. I knew his face made me feel weak in the knees. It was too bad he had breath that could kill.

"Do I need to announce myself or is the clunking of my feet sufficient?" I asked. Though these boots were quieter, more stealthy than my heavy sandals, I was sure he could hear a pin drop in a forest. He was just that type of guy.

"Nah. You walk plenty loud." *Was that an insult?* I couldn't decide if it felt like one or not. I looked down at my shoes.

"I'll try to keep it down over here," I said, rolling my eyes. Not that he saw, because his back was still to me. He had one of his hands on a rope, the other petting the horse who was attached to it.

"This is Penny. She likes beginners because they think the secret to horseback riding is giving plenty of carrots." He reached into a pouch attached to the saddle and pulled out a bag of colorful carrots. "Truth is, I agree. Nothing wrong with treating a horse right." He finally turned to me. Seeing him face to face beat looking at him through a window. The power of our eye contact made my heart feel like it was a tennis ball at Wimbledon. "Do you want to try?" He held out the bag of carrots, and I nodded. Rhett could have been holding a ribbon dancer, and I would have obliged. Slowly taking the bag, in case I might upset Penny with sudden movements, I reached in and handed her one. Her chomps made me laugh.

"Aww. She is so sweet, isn't she?" I felt at peace with the animal I would now have to trust enough to ride.

"I'm Rhett Reed," he said, holding out his hand to shake mine, which required walking a step closer. Into death breath territory. I bet on top of the garlic and onions, he smelled like stale coffee, too.

"Sadie Clark." I shook his hand, shocked at the stark difference from Tommy. Ugh, I did not want to think about Tommy! But his handshake felt soft. Weak. Lame. Rhett had tough hands. He'd worked with them for a living, that was clear. Tommy had never had to hold a rope in his life, let alone earn any callouses or toughen up his skin.

"It's nice to meet you," he said, his expression softening a little as we shook hands. After a minute, my hand was still in his. Sure, I was off in la-la land, comparing the feel of his hands vs. Tommy's, but what was his excuse? We both stiffened up and let go.

"Let's do this, huh?" I asked, trying to be brave. Truthfully, I was fearful of the horse. Yes, Penny was adorable. She had big, brown spots that looked like cappuccinos all over her bright cream fur. Her saddle looked pristine: soft, brown leather that had been expertly crafted. It was mostly the heights and the trust that I was having trouble with. After all, she was an animal. A living being with a mind of her own.

"She said it." Rhett handed me Penny's rope, and motioned to a small set of portable steps behind me, walking past me to retrieve them. I ended up catching a whiff of him. He smelled like pine trees and leather. It was divine. Ugh, I thought.

I let my guard down. But the realization his breath most likely did not reek was obvious. I needed another plan to ensure that I could keep my feelings at bay and this relationship professional.

Then, it dawned on me: *Who said this guy was even single? Surely, if he had a girlfriend, that would sober up my attraction.* Pat said she hoped he would marry, but she didn't say he was single! I would never want to be that woman, pining away for a man who wasn't mine. *There*, I thought. *That would turn it off. Whew! Crisis averted.*

As he picked up the wooden steps and set them near Penny, he motioned for me to walk on them.

"Now, you want to put your left foot in this stirrup, and swing your right leg over, all while holding onto the saddle horn right here." I started as he said, holding onto the saddle horn and putting my foot in the stirrup. "Wrong foot," he said, and I realized I had my right foot in. I took it out, standing firmly back on the step. My heart was still beating out of control. Taking a deep breath, I looked around the small corral. Suddenly, I was filled with panic. *Surely, there was nothing that could get out of control in this little pen, was there?* My mind was racing. I realized I was afraid of trying.

"Cut," I said, putting my hands up in the air. "I just need a moment." Rhett looked at me with a blank expression.

"Take all the time you need," he said, standing still. Patient. Handling whatever this was that I was experiencing. Looking at Penny, I realized I wasn't afraid of her. She was sweet. Calm. Docile. My body began to relax a little.

I grabbed the saddle horn again, and this time, put my left leg in the stirrup. Even with the steps, it was a little high off the ground. Still, I stood there with one leg in the stirrup for a few minutes while I worked up the nerve to swing the other leg over.

After a few attempts that I abandoned part of the way through, I finally lifted myself up long enough to see that I could swing my leg over easily. But once I was in the air, the heights made me feel woozy, and I came tumbling back down.

Rhett caught me mid-fall with his hands, his grip firmly around my waist. His face was next to mine with him behind me. He pushed me forward gently, so I could stand back up on my own.

"Are you alright?" A burst of freshly brushed minty goodness came my way as he spoke. *Of course, he has good breath.* It was really too bad he wasn't single, because he was quite attractive, strong, and had great hygiene. It was at this moment I realized I was spiraling in my attraction to a stranger. I had never felt such a strong physical attraction to a man before Tommy, but now with Rhett, I was really on a disturbing path. *Lord, please keep lust from my heart.*

"I'm a little... disoriented," I said, fully referring to the fact that his handsome appearance was too distracting for me to get any meaningful training here.

"I understand it can be disorienting," he said, and I wondered if he knew he had this effect on women? He then gave me a smile, showing his sparkling, white, minty mouthwash smile. *Of course, he does.* This was another moment for prayer if I'd ever seen one.

Lord, give me the focus to learn this. After all, I'm here to film a movie to get my career back on track, not fall in love with a cowboy.

"Let's try again," I said, stepping back on the portable wooden stairs and putting my left foot in the stirrup. A position that I'd now practiced for so many minutes, it was comfortable to be here. I could do high kicks with this leg, later, after training it to be propped up like this. I took a deep breath, stood with all my weight in the stirrup, and quickly swung the right leg over. I did it. I was in the saddle!

"Great job," Rhett said, giving a flat smile.

"Thank you. For your patience while I got up here. All the way up here…" After the rush of getting in the saddle quickly dissipated, I realized just how high up I felt. I didn't love it. Putting the back of my hand to my forehead was a cliche, but I felt like I may faint from the shock.

"I'm right here. You are safe with me," Rhett said, as he put his hand on my arm, steadying me. His other hand firmly held Penny's rope. Just the words were enough to calm my overactive mind. Rhett wasn't going to let anything happen. Rhett was a strong, capable, *real* cowboy who knew his way around a horse!

"Thank you. I'm ready to, uh, trot, or whatever." Rhett nodded, as he slowly started to walk Penny around the corral.

CHAPTER 9

Rhett

In school, I remembered learning about *Helen of Troy,* during a segment on Greek Mythology. Legend said that she was so beautiful, the Trojan War broke out over her.

I remembered not being able to picture a woman who could look this beautiful. Sure, I'd seen some lookers in my day, on television and movies. But most of that wasn't real. Makeup. Plastic surgery. And beautiful outsides rarely matched what was inside. Sadie was the exception to that. Now, when I wondered what Helen may have looked like, I'd compare it to me seeing Sadie for the first time. If only she wasn't here for just the movie and leaving when she was done.

Her lesson started out pretty rocky. I could barely make eye contact with her without forgetting what we were even doing. While I knew she was panicking, I took the extra time and used it to get a grip on myself. These Hollywood people were used to everything being at their fingertips. The world was their oyster. In that scenario, I was just the sea kelp on the ocean floor. She was here to learn how to look like a real Wyoming woman, and then she was through with me. The thoughts ran ragged through my head, and I began to wonder if this was from God, or the enemy.

Lord, I pray for discernment, and the strength to be professional in this moment, as I lead the most beautiful woman I've ever seen around this horse corral. Please keep my thoughts and heart pure.

If that prayer didn't help, nothing would.

"Ready to pick up some speed?" I asked Sadie, who was starting to look comfortable, mounted in the saddle. Almost, anyway. She was still white knuckling the saddle horn, despite my leading Penny around with the rope.

"Uh, okay." Her hesitancy was sweet. She was fearful; I knew that. But she was doing a great job of pushing through it.

"Let's bump it up to second gear," I said, picking up speed as I walked around. Sadie let out a small yelp but quickly laughed. "You good?" She nodded. Or maybe it was the bumping of her in the saddle that made it look like she was nodding.

"Woah, woah," she hollered out, and Penny came to a slow. I stopped in my tracks.

"Do you need a break?" I asked.

"No, I'm good. I've just heard that in westerns, and I wanted to know if it worked," she laughed, pleased with herself for her horse speak. I took this moment to tuck Penny's lead rope into the front of the saddle. We started back up again, and this time, I stood in the middle of the corral while she went in circles around me. Penny knew what to do. I trusted Penny with the littlest of children—I could trust her with Sadie. Sadie didn't seem to notice that I let go of the lead rope, and I wasn't about to point it out.

"You look like you expect Penny to implode."

"With the amount of westerns I've watched in the last week, I don't want to rule that out as a possibility. Things can get freaky out west." She laughed again, and I basked in the glorious sound. Being around her felt good. Natural. Right. Was this just her "star power," or was it something more?

"Rhett!" A cry came from the lodge, followed by the pattering of little feet that started running toward me.

"Hi, Gracie," I called out to my niece, whom I didn't even know was visiting this weekend. Sadie looked concerned as Penny picked up her speed once more, and she finally noticed I was no longer holding the lead rope.

"Rhett?" she cried out, echoing Gracie as she kept screaming my name as she ran.

"Woah, Penny," the magic words that Sadie repeated as soon as I said them. In a moment, they were stopped, with Penny looking to me for a carrot. All three ladies wanted my attention, as Gracie started to climb the gates of the corral. At just four years old, she could probably make it, judging by her strength and sheer will, but I also didn't want her to fall and hurt herself. I put my hand up to Penny and Sadie, letting them know I'd be right back, ran to the other side of the corral, and snatched Gracie from her climbing.

"Rhett," she said, hugging my neck so tight, I thought I might choke. "Daddy said you'd be here."

"And where is your daddy?" I asked, knowing my brother showing up unannounced meant one of two things; he'd decided he missed Wyoming, or he wanted to see the movie production in action. I snickered at how obvious it was the latter.

"He's talking to Grandma. Mommy isn't here. Mommy is sick." She started to cry. A pit formed in my stomach. Sick? Or, *sick,* sick?

I sat Gracie down next to the corral gates. "Be a good girl for just a minute and stay put, okay?" I asked, and she nodded. Turning back to Sadie, she managed to swing her leg back over the saddle, but without the step below, she was dangling and looking for a place to set her foot. I ran over to her with the steps.

"Sorry about that," I said, motioning back to my niece with my head.

"That's okay. She's a cute one, isn't she?" Her eyes lit up. There were two kinds of people in this world: those who loved kids and wanted some of their own, and those who didn't notice children. The latter didn't hate them but didn't see that role for themselves. I wasn't sure where I lined up until Gracie came into the world. She was the best thing that happened for my brother, but just how much she loved me let me know that having my own someday would be the greatest gift in the world. Seeing Sadie light up at the sight of Gracie made my heart leap.

"The prettiest little girl in the world, and she knows it." We watched Gracie for a moment as she stood by the gate, wearing flare jeans and cowgirl boots with a paisley blouse and pigtails.

My mother, Pat, appeared on the walkway. "There you are, Gracie," she said, with an apologetic look on her face. "I'm sorry to interrupt your lesson, Sadie." Opening the gate, Gracie ran to my mother who picked her up.

"Just a second, Mom," I hollered out before she left back to the lodge. "Just Wyatt here? Gracie said something about her mom being sick."

"She just got her wisdom teeth out. Wyatt thought they'd give her a few days of peace and quiet to recover," my mother laughed.

"Isn't that sweet of Wyatt?"

"Daddy said we could see a movie in real life," Gracie added.

"Did he, now?" I couldn't hold back my laughter. Sadie didn't miss a beat.

"I'm sure you can watch us shoot the movie," she replied graciously, and I was reminded of the fact that Sadie was just here for a few weeks—barely a month. No matter my attraction to her, or the fact that my brother had suddenly appeared, I had a job to do, and that meant she needed to get to riding this horse again.

*****

After we wrapped up another round of riding around in the corral, with Sadie getting on and off the saddle without help, I called it a day.

"Great job, Sadie. It's tradition that I give all of my students a reward after their lesson." I held out a wrapped strawberry candy. She looked at it quizzically before accepting it. "Note that most of my students are young children or very fearful adults; both demographics welcome sugar."

"Surprisingly, this is just what I need." She took the candy, unwrapped it, and popped it into her mouth of sparkling white teeth.

"Tomorrow, we can leave the corral. There's a little trail out here in the field that follows the creek. No inclines, space to roam. I think you'll enjoy it." Her eyes lit up, but there was a tiredness to them.

"That sounds lovely. I hope it is not too early tomorrow. I think we will start filming at nine." She stifled back a yawn just talking about it.

"How about I take you out in the afternoon? After lunch. My mom likes to serve all of the guests in the lodge around one."

"It's a date."

CHAPTER 10

Sadie

I headed back to my cabin after my riding lesson. My legs were so sore and stiff already; I was not excited for what I'd feel like tomorrow. The clawfoot tub was calling my name.

Turning on the faucet, I found a fluffy, white robe hanging on the back of the bathroom door. Two bottles of lavender bubble bath ready to pour in the piping hot water. The scent was so intoxicating, I ended up dumping both bottles in, hoping that was something that would be refilled for me tomorrow.

As I soaked in the wonderful, bubbling water, I thought of the last few weeks of my life. I thought of how God had orchestrated this movie deal for me. This situation had God written all over it, after all.

After a long soak, which resulted in me falling asleep amid the bubbles and waking up in a cold tub of water, my teeth were chattering. Getting out, I dug through my suitcase and found a long sleeve flannel shirt that I wore over a tank top, some boyfriend jeans, and my sandals. The warmth of the day was leaving as the sun began to set. I looked at the clock. Dinner would be served soon. Pat was sure to make me feel welcome to come down to the dining room whenever I wished, as she said she always had food out. I decided to go that way.

In the dining room, the large table was set for dining, family style. Platters of food were everywhere, from heaping bowls of mashed potatoes with chives and sour cream mixed in, roasted green beans with almonds and glistening pats of butter, to macaroni and cheese with a bread crumb topping. Several large bowls of salad lined down the center of the table.

Pat came strolling out of the large, restaurant-style kitchen wheeling a cart that was topped with plates of steak, with those plastic picks they serve you with at restaurants to tell you the temperature the steaks were cooked at.

"Good evening, Sadie." Her face lit up. "I hope you came hungry. Have a seat wherever you like. I'm about to ring the dinner bell." I thought I was still full from lunch, but the aromas changed my mind.

Once she wheeled the cart over to the table, the steam rising off of the piping hot steaks just pulled off the grill, she went to the front door of the lodge, to the left of the kitchen. Reaching upward, she grabbed hold of a rope that I didn't notice before. When she pulled it back and forth, a loud bell rang, echoing in the valley.

Within seconds, people started flowing in, pulling out chairs, talking loudly. Ranch workers and crew members—sitting together at the table like this was how things had always been.

I was the last one to be hired on this movie, since the original actress was laid up in Texas with a broken leg from an unrelated horse incident. My mind shuttered at the thought of how that could happen. Most of the cast and crew had already been here for a few days, if not a week. So tonight, I really stuck out like a sore thumb.

Everyone wanted to sit next to me or talk to me throughout dinner, asking me how I was liking Wyoming so far, as if these fellow Hollywood Californians had any stake to claim in this part of the country. I told them all the same thing: I love it here. I hadn't spent a full day here yet, but this was definitely a place I was looking forward to spending for the next several weeks. Pat twisted a crank and opened the large picture windows, until we were all blasted with the crisp evening air. The smell of a campfire loomed in the distance.

A handful minutes into dinner, Rhett walked in the door. Cleaned up. Fresh clothes. Not a spec of dirt anywhere on the man. He spoke to his mother, Pat, for a few minutes and both of them were grinning ear to ear. There were only a few seats left at the long table, and my heart skipped a beat wondering if Rhett was going to take the seat directly across from me, or the one four seats down on the same side. The latter would have been hard to look at. I sighed. *That's probably a good thing,* I told myself, just as he took the seat out of my view.

Molly's words tumbled through my head about falling in love out here. That was certainly not my intention. I looked around at the table, feeling extremely blessed to be in such good company. This was all such a gift, and despite an intense attraction to Rhett, I needed to put that behind me so I could focus my efforts on this movie. This production deserved my all, and I wanted to give it to them.

As I ate the most wonderful, savory, and tender steak I'd ever had, Pat came by and set fresh pitchers of her famous lavender lemonade on the table. I poured myself a heaping glass, downing it almost immediately. I certainly was thirstier out here, just like Billy said.

As dinner began to wind down, Pat chimed a butter knife on a wine glass to make an announcement.

"Tonight's entertainment will be held outside around the fire, where we will all be blessed by the musical stylings of our very own Rhett." My heart skipped a beat. Rhett was a musician? "If you'd like a dessert, I have chocolate ganache cake, lemon bars, and of course, we have homemade marshmallows to roast over the fire." My excitement amplified.

There were few things in life I enjoyed eating more than marshmallows. Despite them being a sugary, carb-filled confection that I knew better than to eat in large quantities, they were sort of my one sneaky, guilty pleasure in my pantry. After long days on set, or working out, or anything in between, my favorite thing to do was put a marshmallow on a graham cracker and zap it in the microwave for fifteen seconds. But I was ashamed to say I'd never tasted a homemade marshmallow. I nearly jumped at the chance.

"Pat," I said, tapping her on the shoulder while everyone started filtering out of the dining room. She turned to me with a smile.

"Yes, dear?"

"Where do I put my plate?" I was holding the heavy restaurant style plate in my hands. She smiled and shook her head, taking it from me.

"You leave it where you ate, okay sweetheart? We worry about the cleanup around here. You just have a good time." Her words were so genuine, so kind, I couldn't help myself. I hugged her.

"Thank you for dinner. That was the best meal I've had since lunch."

I followed the group outside, pulling my flannel tighter over my body. The sun had almost entirely set; a small glow outlining the ridgeline was all that remained of today's light. The longer I looked at the stunning, sharp peaks, the more they darkened.

"You coming, Sadie?" I turned, seeing it was Billy. When I looked back, the sun was gone.

"Yes. I'm all set," I laughed. We walked together to the fire pit a dozen yards away.

"There's nothing like a Wyoming sunset. Unless of course, you see the sunrise." His words felt like magic.

"What time does it rise? I think I'll need to watch that tomorrow." Billy smiled.

"Dawn is getting a little earlier every day for another month. I'd say about 5:45 is a great time to watch it. It rises from the East. And when it reaches over the tops of those mountains, boy, it will make even the most hardened atheists into believers."

We reached the fire pit, and Billy motioned to an Adirondack chair with a blanket over the back of it for me to sit on.

"You've really thought of everything," I said, pulling the blanket over my lap as the chill of the night felt stronger.

"Up here in the mountains, it's been known to snow every month of the year. You can never be too prepared." He smiled and went to sit on the other side of the fire pit with his granddaughter, whom I guessed was beside his son, judging by the resemblance to Rhett.

Rhett's brother wasn't as rugged as him. He reminded me more of a guy back in Hollywood. More of a city type. He looked like a doting father, though, to his precious daughter, who already had her hands sticky with marshmallows.

The crackling light of the fire had me in a trance as I waited for everyone else to sit down. Pat came out with pouches of marshmallows and roasting rods. I graciously accepted one, eager to try it for myself. As I reached into the pouch and found not just marshmallows but pieces of gourmet chocolate and fancy, circular-shaped graham crackers, Rhett appeared, sitting at the fire directly across from me, and adding a large log to the flames, increasing the height. Almost making it hard for me to see above the flames to him. Almost.

Reminding myself of my earlier pact to do the best job I could for this movie, and not get distracted, I went back to my marshmallows. Putting two on the roasting stick, I held it out in the flame, trying everything I could to keep my eyes on my little treat and not look up. That lasted all of five seconds, and the second I did look up, my eyes met Rhett's. And he was looking at me.

The guitar strap was slung over his black Carhartt coat. He donned a crisp, clean black cowboy hat that looked like it was cut just for his head. My thoughts went back to Tommy's hat collection that he bought off of western hat dealers. Each one was more expensive than the last. Though I didn't know what something like that should cost, I had the sneaking suspicion Tommy was getting robbed blind because of his sheer... desperation... to look like a cowboy.

Now, as I looked at a *real* cowboy in front of me, my hand started to feel warm as I remembered I was actively roasting a marshmallow, not having a staring contest. I pulled my roasting rod out of the fire, but it was too late. It was doused in flames, black as coal, and melting off the stick. *Drats.*

"Does anyone else want marshmallows?" Pat called out, just in time. I stood.

"I'll take more, if that's okay. Mine got a little too... uh, cooked." Pat nodded, walking over to me and handing me a fresh bag.

"Don't overcook these ones. Stay focused on the task at hand," she said, giving me a wink. Oh, my word, was I *that* obvious? A blush rose to my cheeks as I considered the fact that everyone knew I was crushing on the hot cowboy sitting across from me. Just another reason I needed to straighten up. After all, my reputation was already more than a little hazy. What would happen if word got out that I liked another guy? *Never mind the fact that I didn't even know him!*

I crawled back into my Adirondack chair, bending my legs so I could put my feet on the seat. I shoved an uncooked, cold marshmallow into my mouth just to regain a sense that I was cool. Unbothered. Not worried about what anyone thought of me. The sweet, sugary confection grabbed a hold of my senses like Pat rang the dinner bell. The spike to my blood stream made me feel like anything was possible. Rhett strummed the first chord to a song, bringing a lump to my throat as he started to sing the most beautiful, emotional, and cowboy version of *Amazing Grace.*

His voice was better than anything I'd ever heard. Not polished. Not flashy. Just deep and worn in, and like it was used to being carried throughout this valley.

At that first chord, when he broke into the song, singing the first words, *"Amazing grace,"* everyone fell silent. Even Gracie, who had marshmallows stuck on her cheeks, nose, and albeit all over her fingers that splayed themselves around her dads neck, stopped moving to listen to her uncle sing. *"How sweet the sound."*

It was a song I'd heard a hundred times. In church pews. In movies. At funerals for family. But I'd never heard it like this. With Rhett, the song had a new body of emotional depth that I didn't think possible. A lump formed in the back of my throat. I didn't know how not to cry right now.

Rhett's eyes were either closed, while he reached deep inside himself to strum the song and sing the words, or they were glued to the flames. He wasn't singing for us, though he had the full, undivided attention of everyone around the large stone firepit. No, it was clear with each strum of the guitar that Rhett was singing for God. The Holy Spirit was here—the presence filling everyone around. I basked in the glory, thanking God for this song, this company, this musician who had more gifts than he knew.

When he was done with the song, the fire popped loudly, breaking the silence that had formed over the group of people. His mom, Pat, was the first to speak, and she unapologetically wiped tears from her eyes.

"That was beautiful, Rhett." Others followed in their praise.

CHAPTER 11

Rhett

No matter how many times I sat around this fire and ang to our guests, it never got any easier to accept the compliments. Truth was, I was singing for Jesus. This group of guests were a little more in tune to that than others, thankfully.

The firepit serenading ended after a few more songs. Everyone had an early rise time tomorrow, including myself. My parents, brother and niece wandered off to their beds. The crew trickled out, and Sadie, in the mix of people, stood. I expected myself to work up the nerve to say something to her, but I couldn't. I needed to hold that boundary. She was here to work, and I was here to help her do that. The time would be over before we both knew it, and back to Hollywood she would go.

I noticed as Sadie wrapped the blanket tight around her shoulders. She was cold in this mountain air. I pictured putting my arm around her to warm her up, before quickly batting that idea away. *This was going to be a couple of weeks*, I thought. After all, we were just two perfect strangers, and she was already filling up way too much space in my head for someone I didn't even know.

Normally, I'd draw a bucket of sand over this fire and call it a night. But something was telling me to stay, as I sat with the fire lowering naturally. Sadie walked to her cabin, shutting the door behind her. I couldn't help but notice the lights inside remained on. She was still awake. Here I was, thinking of her. Was she thinking of me, too?

Before I knew it, I was alone at the firepit. Staring at a woman's cabin like I was some sort of a weirdo. I shook my head, putting it in my hands as I said a prayer. "Lord, please help get my head on straight."

The fire dwindled down to nothing. It had nowhere to go, and the wind wasn't blowing. The air was perfectly calm and dry. I still sprinkled a little bit of sand over the top, putting out what was left of the gentle burn, before turning into my own living quarters.

*****

My cabin was a log, two-bedroom home that I built myself the summer I turned eighteen. Out here on the ranch, I was situated up the river. Away from the guest cabins. Away from what little noise our ranch produced. My parents had deeded me the small acreage when I was just a teen, breaking off two parcels for both me and my brother. Though he never built on his, I couldn't wait to stake my claim.

My cell phone, though rarely used, was flashing with notifications when I returned to my house. First things first, I pulled off my boots, sitting in the chair by the door to do it. Pouring myself a large glass of water from the apron sink, I thought about how this house was a smattering of building supplies that I could afford at eighteen, and that I was able to find at the local hardware store and around the ranch. This particular sink always reminded me of my grandparents, as they salvaged it from their first home out here that later burned down.

After the fire, they were getting up there in age and spent the rest of their years living in the main lodge for ease. Truthfully, I thought neither one of them recovered from the heartbreak of losing their home, and they never cared to build another one.

My grandmother, Cora Lynn, always said it was her dream sink, but never explained why. When I asked her, she would just tell me that one day, when I'm married, my wife will feel the same way.

Putting my glass in the sink, I turned back to my phone, which was gently buzzing with news of something. Opening the screen, the social media app that frankly, I had forgotten I had, popped up with notifications for the first time in years. *47 new likes.*

Tapping on the app, my mind wandered: *Could this be from Sadie?*

"Who is Molly?" I asked aloud, to an empty house. Shrugging it off, I sat down on my recliner and typed *Sadie Clark* in the search bar. Hundreds of results came back within seconds. Images of her and a man wearing a Stetson that was too large for his head popped up first. Sadie, at an award show, wearing a very beautiful leather dress. More images of that night, including several that looked like they were taken through a set of rhododendrons by some secret spy, of Sadie and the

Stetson kissing. Or, more like him holding her up to him with a white knuckle death grip and her not being able to get away.

Before I knew it, I read several articles about Sadie and this chump, Tommy, who apparently dumped her right after this. Eyewitnesses said she did not go into his house with him that night. I'd never been particularly good with math, but one plus one did not equal five. It was clear to me, a half-witted country bumpkin that knew more about horses than women, that Tommy was a jerk who decided he wanted a woman who would go home with him. Why the rest of the movie industry was taking his side was beyond me. Sadie had more acting talent in her pinky than this guy did in his whole body.

I shouldn't have done it. But after I put the phone down, I got curious. I pulled up my computer. Booting it up sounded like it might overheat, and the computer's fans turned on full blast. I hadn't used this thing much over the years, and it had just been collecting dust in my second bedroom. The phone was hard for me to read on, however. I needed a larger screen with a keyboard so that I didn't fat finger every letter.

Going down the Tommy Wheeler rabbit hole, I discovered he played a cowboy on that television show that some of our guests said inspired their trip out west. I hadn't ever seen it, as I didn't watch much television. But I did have one, and the last time I checked, the cable out here was working. Once I found the show's schedule, I realized the next episode was starting in about five minutes. I turned off my computer that, sighing in relief back at me, shut down like it may have never turned back on again, went back into my living room, and put on the channel.

The opening scene had a montage of Tommy running his horse for what appeared to be many miles and hours at a time. I was already feeling annoyed, as you couldn't run a horse like that. If he did that for real for an hour, he'd be carryin' his saddle home. Sure, they could do explosive spurts of distances, but realistically, that would exhaust a horse. Most of the riding was a good trot. And that was just the truth.

Then, when he did slow, he was bouncing. Not absorbing the movements but gripping the saddle like he was trying to pop a balloon with his knees.

At the end of this scene—one that couldn't have come soon enough—he got out of the saddle, completely disregarding the horse that he appeared to just have been riding for hours. All he did was loop the lead about a dead tree in a barren land. No food, no water. No checking the legs for swelling. No animal welfare whatsoever. I'd seen more care from my neighbors who raised raccoons than the first five minutes of this racket. I really didn't like this show.

As I watched his character move about and have a discussion with other actors, I couldn't help but feel biased against everything he did. Yet, he was certainly not a good actor. All I saw when I looked at him was a guy pretending to be like the people out here in the real American West. This guy couldn't survive a winter on the range. Let alone a pack trip in the mountains if it rained and got his Stetson wet. After a few more minutes of watching, I had to turn off the television. *Lord, please don't let me stoop to this guy's level.* I did not wish to hate anyone. Jesus commanded us to love our enemies. This guy, heck, this show, was making that hard to do, so I needed to pause and reflect.

CHAPTER 12

Sadie

The moment I got back to my cabin, I had to close the windows. The chill was making my teeth chatter. Rhett was still sitting out by the firepit when I walked off. It was nearly 9 at night—time to hit the hay. I was completely wiped out from my big schedule and tomorrow, I would be rising pretty early to get ready for filming. There was also a sunrise I wanted to see.

Still, I couldn't just end the day without checking in with my people. I still hadn't let my parents know I'd arrived at my new filming location. I hadn't told Janie that I was pleased as punch with my living arrangements. I hadn't told Molly that the cowboy played guitar.

Quickly sending a message to my parents, and an email to my agent, Janie, I moved onto Molly.

Me: Molly. The cowboy plays guitar and can sing (Amazing Grace) like it's the language of my heart. Please advise.

Molly: Excuse me—a real cowboy? Who sings... worship music?

Molly: Sadie Clark, if you fumble this, I will be gravely disappointed.

Molly: Also

Molly: What is the cowboy's name?

Me: Why? Don't tell me you want to stalk him on the internet. Heck, I don't even know *if* he's on the internet.

Molly: I promise I'll be good. I just need a first, last, and social security number to be sure.

Me: Very funny. I don't know if I'm spelling it right, but his name is Rhett Reed.

Molly: Of course it is.

Me: It even sounds like a cowboy name.

Molly: He's on here, all right.

Me: On where?

Molly: I thought you were taking a sabbatical from social media? I don't want this to tempt you out of it.

As I contemplated things for a moment, Molly was right. I decided I wasn't going to be on the apps while I was filming. Besides, every time I logged on, reminders of Tommy and his slimy lies filled my screen. I didn't need that right now.

Me: You're right. Don't tell me. In fact, don't even tell me what details you uncover, because I really need to focus on filming. This cowboy is not the distraction I need. And my reputation may falter even further if it gets out just how hot I think he is.

Molly: Aha! So, you admit that he's hot, eh?

Me: I better get to sleep. Early morning tomorrow.

Molly: Go to bed, Sadie. And pray for discernment.

Molly: And that his forearms are really as strong as they look.

When I plugged in my phone, put it on silent, and turned off the lights, I did just that as I climbed into bed. Well, the first part, anyway. Mostly, I prayed for those around me and those back home and in Hollywood. I prayed for Tommy, too. He hurt me, yes, but I was shocked at the lies coming from a man who claimed to be a believer. I didn't know that Tommy had a real relationship with Jesus, so I started there. As I drifted off to sleep, I also prayed that I would be able to wake in time for the sunrise with how tired I felt. That I could get a restful sleep. That I could be as rested as possible for my very long day tomorrow... That included a date, er, horseback riding lesson, with Rhett.

*****

I woke up three minutes before my alarm went off, thanking God for my answered prayers as I sat up from the bed, feeling extremely rested. Ready to go. Something about this fresh mountain air made me sleep like a rock. Better than I had in years. I reset the alarm on my phone so it wouldn't alert me again until tomorrow.

I pulled on my thick flannel shirt from last night over my white and pink tank top and pajama pants set. Matching slippers slid over my thick wool socks—the real kind, made from people who shear sheep on the highest mountain tops. I may have been enjoying the glitz and glam of acting, but my biggest splurge on myself wasn't fancy clothes, shoes, or cars. It was wooly socks that came with pictures of the sheep on the label.

I stepped outside, moving as quietly as I could, not wanting to wake anyone on the ranch. It was dark outside, but Billy was right—a glow had already begun behind the mountains. Light was starting to spill onto everything around me. I stepped off my cabin's porch, being lulled over to another set of chairs that had been set up right next to the river. *What a perfect place to sit, even at the crack of dawn,* I thought, taking a seat.

As the light got brighter, I noticed movement around the ranch. People were already up and about. The lights on in the dining hall; Pat must have been preparing breakfast. A stirring in the horse corral; perhaps the horses were being fed. I'd always known that ranchers got up early, but I never thought about why. Now that I was watching the sunrise, I understood; because this sort of beauty, once seen, can never be slept through again.

Walking back to my cabin in my fluffy slippers and flannel, I took a second glance when I saw Rhett out. Fully dressed, ready for the day. Yes, it was technically daytime now that the sun had risen, but it still couldn't be later than half past six. He gave me a second glance, too.

"Good morning?" he asked, looking a little unsure at what I was doing up this early.

"Morning," I said, pulling my flannel a little tighter, as if that would have made my bedhead look better and my unbrushed teeth glossier. "I got up to see the sunrise. Billy told me what time and all." Rhett nodded and held back a smile.

"And what did you think?"

"I'd give it five stars," I said with a smile. "Billy wasn't exaggerating."

"He never does," Rhett said, his eyes fixed on me.

"Well, see you later," I said, scurrying back inside my cabin.

A half hour later, I emerged with brushed hair and teeth and fresh clothes. My makeup team would be doing the rest—I just needed to give them a clean canvas to work with. The first stop was the dining hall. I was greeted by Pat the moment I walked in.

"I hope you like cinnamon rolls," she said with a wink.

"Who doesn't?" I asked, eyeballing the treats that were nearly as big as the plate they sat on. I patted my stomach that was growing fuller every second I was here. "Though I better share that with nine of my closest friends, or I'm not going to fit into my clothes." Pat gave me a nod.

"Well, I figured you might feel that way. I know how it is, and the expectations cast upon you. That's why I made you a small roll that you can eat guilt-free." My eyes widened as she pulled a plate off of a warming rack with the perfectly sized cinnamon roll that served one person only. I couldn't help myself, and I took a huge bite, right then and there. She laughed in delight.

"It's official—I'm moving to the ranch full-time," I said, as I chewed through the deliciously delectable cinnamon roll that was both fluffy and gooey, with a not-too-sweet cream cheese frosting. Pat gave me a surprised smile and looked behind me. I turned to be face-to-face with Rhett. I couldn't describe the look on his face if I tried. It wasn't humorous, nor was it anxious. It was almost a relief. For what, I had no idea.

"Take a plate and help yourself, sweetheart. There is plenty of food around." Pat handed me a large serving plate and pointed me in the direction of a fresh buffet of eggs, bacon, hashbrowns, and more. There were several kinds of coffee— from drip to French press. Even a young man from the kitchen side came wheeling out an espresso machine. Next to the savory items was an entire cart of sweet pastries, oatmeal, and pancakes.

Looking around the room, I noticed that everyone seemed to be eating what they wanted here. Sure, they weren't piling pancakes a mile high and using an entire stick of butter on their waffles, but this didn't feel like someone was watching me like a hawk, expecting me to weigh my food. I didn't feel like someone was going to walk out with a measuring tape to check my waste. Not that either of those things had happened on set before, but it was kind of an unspoken thing that thin was in.

After getting a modest portion of bacon and eggs that I knew I could eat and not let anything go to waste, I requested an espresso from the coffee station. He said he would bring it to me. Turning back to the cafeteria style tables, I had a flashback of high school. Except this time, everyone wanted to sit next to me. I hadn't accidentally left the size sticker on my jeans, and I didn't have too-short bangs that I had cut myself.

I smiled as Tonya, from the movie crew, motioned for me to sit next to her. As I slid onto the bench, my eyes moved to her plate that *was* piled high with French toast. She busted up laughing.

"I know grains are now passe," she smirked. "And that I'm supposed to be eating protein. But nothing keeps me fuller than eating a loaf of bread, first thing in the morning." We both giggled as she put a piece on my plate to try. Cutting off the smallest piece I could, my eyes widened when it touched my taste buds. The bread was sourdough and had both a syrupy sweetness and a crisp to the outer layer. Biting into it was like eating dessert first, which I already did with the mini cinnamon roll from Pat. This tasted even better.

"Wow," I said, cutting off a larger piece this time.

"I know. Pat makes the bread herself." Tonya was quickly working her way down the stack.

"Is there anything she can't make? My word, the food here is good. This is better than any catering I've ever had on a set." Tonya agreed.

"Because these are all home-cooked meals. Made with love. Sounds cheesy, but you can't argue that." As I chewed through the rest of my sourdough French toast and finished my eggs and bacon, I looked over at Pat who was studiously working to hand out cinnamon rolls. They were already almost gone.

CHAPTER 13

Sadie

"Lights... Camera... Cut!" The director stood from his chair. We were just about to shoot our very first scene, and my hands were sweating with nerves. I was practicing my lines, but I had to learn them all on the fly, and this particular scene had complicated dialogue. For once, I was pleased with putting it off for another few minutes and immediately pulled out my script that I had hid behind the old whiskey barrel and started re-reading. Chatter was happening all around me, but I didn't pay any attention until he came up and was a few feet away. "What is that?" He pointed to the ground next to my feet. I glanced down and nearly fainted from the fright.

"Don't tell me it's another poshly dressed raccoon!" Someone yelled from behind the set.

"No, it's a rattlesnake!" Screams ensued. People scrambled. And then there was me, immobilized by the fear of getting bitten to the point where I thought if I didn't move, it couldn't see me. Or was that dinosaurs?

"Sadie, don't make any sudden movements," Peter, another one of the director's assistants, called out to me. Someone walked over with a shotgun that looked more real than a movie prop, and I started to feel like I was about to topple over. Here I was, wearing a puffy, long-sleeved blouse, with a corset and heavy skirt that wasn't very good for having a panic attack in, and this happened. Thankfully, Billy appeared from around a corner holding some sort of wire contraption that looked like it was for catching dogs.

In one fell swoop, he snatched up the rattle snake and walked off with it. Everyone was still running circles around the set, while my knees buckled, and I sat down for a moment, fanning my face with the script.

"Carry on," Mark, the director, finally said after getting back into his chair as if nothing happened. I set my script down again, behind the whiskey barrel that was now holding up my entire body weight and cleared my throat.

"Lights. Camera," Mark paused, looking all around the ground of the set, as if there may be more snakes. Everyone followed his lead, while I looked straight ahead, into the camera. "Action."

*****

"You *nailed* that, Sadie!" Peter came up and gave me a high five after the scene was over. "Even that little twang to your voice. We didn't even discuss that, and honestly, we don't have a budget for a dialogue coach, so I know everyone's thrilled that you've taken it upon yourself to sound authentic." I nodded, thanking him.

"Thanks, Peter. It just sort of came out. I... I didn't really think about it beforehand, either." Peter's jaw dropped.

"You're a real one, Sadie." Peter walked off, and I let out a breath. The scene went well. Not perfect, but I managed to stumble through my lines. The "twang" Peter referred to was just from my own nerves. I said a prayer of thankfulness to the Lord, as Tonya walked over with a clipboard.

"Sadie, the next scene has you on the horse, in a saddle. But you are not going anywhere just yet. Are you comfortable with that?" Nerves hit me like a shockwave. But if it was Penny, I was comfortable. She was as trustworthy as Rhett said.

"Yes, I am. But can I request the horse I rode yesterday?" Before I could even answer, Rhett appeared, leading Penny to me with a rope.

"Where do we want her?" he asked, looking at Tonya who smiled and blushed. It was clear I wasn't the only woman subject to his good looks.

"Right over here. On the other side of the saloon." Tonya pointed to the edge of our set, which was perfectly set up in this vast, open field. Viewers would never know that just to the left of it was a real working guest ranch with cabins, animals, and a massive river. And real cowboys. The kind that weren't made up by some Hollywood script.

"Is this okay?" Tonya turned back to me once Rhett walked away, as if the spell of his charms had been broken.

"With that horse? Yes." I was pleased to see it was Penny. She would also look beautiful on camera.

"Wonderful. We will give you some time to get comfortable in the saddle and then we will start up again." Suddenly, I remembered my outfit.

"Wait," I said, touching Tonya's arm before she walked away. She looked up at me expectantly. "I'm wearing a dress?" Tonya nodded.

"This is a "split riding skirt,' as they called it. A replica, so not entirely authentic, but see this front panel here?" She reached down and motioned to the fabric around my knees, pointing to the buttons. "This part gets unbuttoned. Or, in this case, I think we made it with snap buttons. And then, it's like you're wearing gaucho pants. Do you remember those? Or are you too young? Never mind," she said with a laugh. "I'm really dating myself here. Turning the big 4-0 next month." She trailed off, and I gave her a smile. "May I?" With my permission, she unsnapped the panel. "This protected modesty while riding astride. Otherwise, women were expected to ride side-saddle."

Once the panel was undone, I walked over to Rhett, who had Penny on a lead rope.

"I'm here to take a seat in the saddle," I said, pointing to my hilarious skirt that had now turned into pants.

"I see that," Rhett said, who looked like he was trying to hold back his smile. He already had a stool pulled out for me to step onto, and I wasted no time stepping onto it. Putting my left foot into the stirrup, I swung my right leg over, feeling the muscle soreness from yesterday's riding hit me. Rhett wasted no time adjusting the saddle to my legs.

As he brought up the stirrups an inch on each side, I felt there was nothing more intimate about him fitting me for this scene. His face was hidden by his hat. His hands gently at work while one momentarily held the back of my laced-up boot to better position it. His touch was electrifying. Several minutes went by—Rhett was meticulously ensuring the saddle fit like a glove, and I found myself savoring the time with him.

"I'm going to hand you the rope, so it's not in the scene. But she's not going to go anywhere unless you tell her to." Rhett's deep voice brought me back to reality. I looked around— the crew was ready. Penny and I were in frame. Rufus was holding his clapperboard, with the scene details already scribbled on it. Everyone had been waiting on whatever this was, and my cheeks reddened at the thought that I was being obvious about my attraction to this cowboy. Another reputation buster for me, this soon after my breakup with my short-lived boyfriend. I had to keep it together. I couldn't get lost in his masculinity. His rugged lifestyle. His deep, whiskey barrel voice that when he sang, carried over the campfire and down the mountainous valley.

"Let's roll in three minutes," Peter said, as I took the rope from Rhett's hand.

"I'll be right here," he said under his breath. A fact I found comforting, though I did feel safe with Penny. She was a good horse.

"Thank you," I told him, but I looked straight ahead. This was getting out of hand. Not only did I not know this cowboy, but I was leaving here once filming was done. This wasn't going to ever go anywhere. If it was God's will that I marry one day, I would. I didn't need to be chasing people down in the meantime and daydreaming about what their kiss would feel like with all of that stubble. *Sadie!*

I shook the thought out of my head for the last time. *This is ridiculous.* If only Molly were here. She would talk some sense into me. But then again, she would probably be just as enchanted with this setting, this life. A lightbulb went off in my head. *That's it!* I just liked this place. And because of it, I was feeling extra attraction to this man who happened to live in this place. If I took him out of here and placed him under a palm tree in the Hollywood Hills, would I really feel the same amount of attraction? *Don't answer that,* I told myself.

"Ready?" Tonya called out to Rufus and Peter as she scribbled down a few notes. Those three minutes went by quickly. The crew nodded.

"Lights. Camera..." The clap of the board rang through the valley.

"Yeehaw!" One of my co-stars, Ben Holloway, suddenly came roaring up beside me on a horse. For a second, I worried that Penny might get spooked as he stopped close next to me, but thankfully, Rhett had been right. She didn't move an inch.

"Howdy, ma'am," he said to me. "Can you point a feller in the direction of a tradin' post?" He waited for a beat and put his hand on his hat which was my cue. It was then I nearly forgot my line to respond.

"Just yonder," I pointed back towards the mountain valleys. "But you won't find much worth tradin' if you don't know how to ride proper. This land is riddled with rattlers." *Oh, how true these words were becoming,* I thought.

"I reckon I can manage." Ben grinned at me, and his smile felt real. He tipped his hat and rode off, full speed ahead, into the valley behind.

"Cut!" Rufus called out, and Ben's horse came to a stop.

Rhett appeared at my side again instantly, setting the portable stair down below me. He took the lead rope from my hands, and I released the death grip I had on it.

Kicking my foot out of the stirrup on my right, I swung my leg back over the saddle, meeting the stairs easily.

"Thank you," I said, followed by a curtsy in my balloon pants/skirt combo. He smiled and handed me a strawberry candy. "Do I deserve this just for that scene?" I asked, accepting the candy anyway.

"Any form of bravery deserves a reward." And just like that, he and Penny sauntered off, and I was swarmed with makeup and wardrobe, readying me for the next scene.

CHAPTER 14

Rhett

Seeing Sadie act on the big screen was impactful. Witnessing in person blew me away. Not only was it fun seeing the whole movie set in place, from the old saloon wall, and the props that made it feel like we were standing in the late 1800's, but seeing Sadie in full costume gave me all the feels. I'd always related to the pioneer men; their sense of adventure. Their desire to explore. Sadie would have been the perfect pioneer woman, at least perfectly looking the part.

Now, as I walked Penny back to her pen, I saw the crew prepare a scene where two cowboys would shoot guns. It was clear to me that not one person in this cast or crew had ever even held a gun before, real or fake. I let Penny in her corral and quickly walked over to lend a hand.

"May I step in?" I asked, the whole crew turning to me as I motioned to the gun. Tonya, who was always chatting me up, stepped in.

"Yes, Rhett. We'd love any guidance you can give us to make this feel the most authentic." She batted her eyes. "Ben?" We all looked at Ben, who was still holding the gun, incorrectly at that. Ben relented, nodding and haphazardly handed it to me.

"Woah. Right there. First of all, even if it's not, a gun is *always* loaded," I said, pointing the barrel to the sky.

"You're right, man. My apologies." Ben stood and reached out and shook my hand.

"That's okay. We were all beginners once." I readjusted the gun, aiming it at a hill in front of me. "When you hold it, you want it butted up to your shoulder. The shoulder takes the impact. If it's above your shoulder and you shoot it, you're likely going to miss your target, as it does have a kickback." As I held the Winchester Yellowboy replica, I opened the barrel. Sure enough, it was empty. I closed it and handed it back to Ben.

"How does this look?" Ben was a Hollywood cowboy, through and through. He looked the part on camera, but he didn't know a rope from a rodeo, and that part was apparent.

"Much better. Now, let's work on your aim." After working with Ben and another cowboy who came over to get some pointers, they were in much better straights. Tonya said she would walk me to the horse corral, where I was going to round up a few horses for the next scene.

"Thanks for all the help with the guns," she said, affectionately putting her hand on my bicep. I nodded.

"You're welcome. They needed it. I have to remember not everyone grew up shooting guns from the cradle like I did." Tonya let out an infectious laugh.

"Now that's a movie idea!"

"Don't think any California movie executives would care for that one." I shrugged. Tonya changed the subject.

"You're so much more than a horse consultant. You are also the weapon expert, and I'm going to make sure you get compensated for that role, as well. If you're interested, anyway." I knew the pay wasn't spectacular for the horse consultant, so I couldn't imagine helping with the weapons was even near my time, but the thought of an inaccurate western being filmed on my ranch didn't sit well with me, either.

"I'll do it. Thanks, Tonya." When we reached the horse corral, she excitedly jotted down some notes before being called away by the director. Something about Ben needing his makeup touched up. I rolled my eyes and laughed, reminding myself that if I was in one of these movies, all the makeup in the world couldn't help me.

At the horse corral, my heart sank: Penny was nowhere to be found.

"Penny," I called out, followed by the whistle that let her know treats were near. Then, I saw the culprit: The back gate of the corral was left open. Perhaps my brother took her out? My mom? Dad? I didn't panic. She'd escaped before and managed to get down to the river, her favorite place to get a drink, before turning back. She had some spunk in her, but the reminder that it was summer and rattle snakes were appearing in troves made me that much more nervous.

I started walking the perimeter of the cabins for any sign of her. Then, I found a set of hoof prints that were likely hers, unless someone else had a horse walking around. "Penny?" I called out again, whistling like a maniac. Crew members started walking up to me, asking about the next scene.

"I'm sorry, but my horse is missing. I'll be there as soon as I can," I promised them, understanding that I wasn't the only one involved in this. A lot of money was riding on this movie production—the rates they were paying to rent our ranch alone was enough to pay the wages of our ranch hands for the next two years. It was a fine line from freaking out and looking for my favorite horse, to being a respectful and courteous horse. A line I wasn't riding well.

Thankfully, I encountered my dad on the search.

"Could you do me a favor?" I asked, pleading with my eyes. He nodded immediately.

"Of course, son. What is it?"

"Penny is missing, and the set needs horses for their next scene. Could you take Ranger, Domino, and Ace over to them? They are in the barn and already have their bridles on." He nodded and went right away. "Thanks, Dad."

"Uh huh. Find Penny. We don't need her gettin' into anything," he said, as he quickly hurried to the barn.

About five years ago, we had a horse go missing. We couldn't find him anywhere. He was a smaller horse with big feet. He just never grew into them. We called him Bigfoot.

Bigfoot was missing for over one hundred days. It seemed crazy to think that a horse could vanish on a flat ranch in a mountain valley, but he did. We searched day and night for him for weeks. Though the search party got smaller, we never gave up hope. When he eventually sauntered back into eyesight one day, from a direction we searched every square inch of, he looked like he'd been gone for five minutes. No sign of starvation. No weariness to his body. His feet were a little long—the farrier came that same day. But otherwise, our horse was fine.

A few days later, I retraced his steps the best I could. Found a spot that looked like a horse had been bedding down on. A water source. A field of alfalfa nearby. Bigfoot had been living off the land a handful of miles away, but it was a spot that wasn't completely accessible by foot. You needed to cross the river to get there. Something I'd never expected him to do.

Now, with Penny missing, my mind was racing a million miles an hour imagining the worse. Bigfoot was a great horse, and I missed him, but Penny was *my* horse. There was a difference. I needed to find her now.

On the perimeter search, I was analyzing the ground for hoof prints and anything that could be a sign, when I ran into my brother, Wyatt, and Gracie. I enlisted their help immediately.

"We'll walk to the south end," Wyatt said, picking Gracie up. I nodded.

"Thanks, bro." I kept walking for a second and paused. "Later, I'd like to catch up." Wyatt turned back to face me.

"Sure," he smiled.

"Is everything what you say it is?" I asked him, not sure if I fully understood what he was doing here without his wife. This wasn't exactly normal for him. They'd been joined at the hip since they met. Wyatt's eyes went to Gracie, who was holding a Barbie doll with ragged hair and cowgirl boots. He nodded.

"She just... needed a reset. Some time for her. I wanted her to have it. Especially before we do this all over again." He grinned ear to ear.

"Another one?" I whispered this time, not knowing if Gracie understood she would be getting a sibling. Wyatt nodded.

"She just got her wisdom teeth out. And it's so cute-— she looks like a real chipmunk. But we're hoping... Lord willing, this time next year..." He trailed off.

"I'm happy for you, bro," I said, and I meant it.

"It's going to happen for you, too, Rhett." And with that, he turned away and headed towards the south end of the ranch, looking for Penny.

As I walked, I couldn't get the words out of my head. *It's going to happen for you, too.* I had never let on to anyone that I wanted a family by now. Or, was even ready for a wife. Perhaps it was just *that* obvious? But even if God did send me a partner, it wasn't like that sort of thing happened overnight. You had to get to know a person. Learn about them. Fall in love.

Unless you were my brother, I guessed. He fell in love first and got to know her second. The thought of which had brought me a lot of wonder and confusion over the years. Sure, I had accepted that it happened. And it sure worked out for them. But I just couldn't grasp the idea of it because I hadn't experienced it myself. As I walked, I pondered the ideas of love and what the Lord may or may not have in store for me.

*****

"Rhett?" An angelic voice rang out from behind me. My first instinct was to look up, thinking there was an actual angel, considering I was alone out here, almost to where the river started. At least a mile from the ranch. "Rhett," she said again, and I realized it was Sadie. I spun around and looked at her, unsure why she was here. "I heard Penny was missing, and I wanted to help."

Then, it hit me. I'd been walking all this way for the last half hour, searching for my horse, daydreaming about the Lord, and I didn't have the slightest inclination that someone was walking behind me? I was really starting to lose my touch.

"Thank you," I said with a nod, giving her a once over. She was still in her set costume, with those riding pants that started as a skirt, and wearing familiar cowboy boots. A pair that certainly came from my mother's closet. She'd been known to lend out shoes to ladies who visited the ranch. She even kept a bottle of that aerosol spray sanitizer like they had in bowling alleys to clean them afterwards.

I paused in my movements while Sadie caught up to me. The thoughtfulness of her walking all this way while I was certain she had other things required of her was touching. Suddenly, all of those thoughts about having to get to know someone before falling in love were popping like balloons in my mind.

"Shouldn't you be filming?" I asked, while we walked side-by-side along the crackling, babbling river. She shrugged.

"I just finished my last scene for the day. Technically, we could have filmed one more, but I'm only contracted for what I've already completed. I got surprisingly good terms for this movie. Better than the big productions. It has me thinking I should just do indie films." She let out a little laugh. "It sure is a great location, too." Something about how she said the last part made me wonder if any of that had to do with me. The thought itself was ridiculous—this was Sadie Clark, for crying out loud. While she didn't seem to have an ounce of that shallow, vapid, self-obsession starlet thing going on, she could still have anyone she wanted. She could do whatever she wanted. She could even kiss me right now, and I wouldn't object.

"I think I'm losing it," I said under my breath, the words slipping out like a leak.

"Don't worry." Sadie stopped and put her hand on my arm, where Tonya's had been just a while prior. But Sadie's touch sent electricity through my body. "We will find her." Penny. The task at hand. With my attention refocused, Sadie and I continued to walk the river, chatting idly about Penny, life in Dust Creek, and everything in between. The conversation felt savored by both of us as we got to know each other.

CHAPTER 15

Sadie

There's more to the story, as there usually is.

We were about to shoot one more scene. Then, my manager called. Not me, as my phone was in my cabin. She called Tonya, who then pulled me aside.

"Let's take five," Tonya announced to the crew, while I answered the phone.

"Hello?"

"Sadie, it's Janie. Sorry to call in the middle of filming." She didn't leave me much room for platitudes. "I just wanted to get to you before anyone else could. Listen, it doesn't matter what anyone thinks, okay? This industry is full of a bunch of—,"
I cut her off.

"I missed it. What happened?" The anxiety welling in the back of my mind.

"You haven't been online?" she asked. The tone in her voice told me she wasn't aware she was now going to be the messenger of whatever new drama this was.

"No. After everything, I'm taking a social media sabbatical."

"That's good. Okay, then. Well, never mind, in that case. Get back to filming, and—," I cut her off again.

"Just tell me, Janie. What happened?" She let out a sigh.

"Tommy posted a photo of you and implied that..." Janie trailed off.

"Implied *what?*" My heart raced.

"Implied that... Things happened between you. Physical things. And since I know you and respect your commitment to purity, I—." For a moment, I blacked out. I could no longer hear the words she was saying. I just stammered out the only words I could.

"What photo?"

"You are in bed, with a tray on your lap that has food on it." My face went hot. My mouth was dry. Tears welled in my eyes.

"That was when I had that awful sinus infection after doing the perfume ad. They thought I should also smell the part, as if people have *smell-o-vision* on their television sets."

"Tommy is such a—," Janie stopped short.

"He insisted on bringing me that soup. Then he said I looked so cute, and he wanted to take a picture. I smiled at him. That was genuine. Little did I know, he would be using that against me now. But I just have one question..." I couldn't believe this was happening.

"Don't worry, we can make a statement on your behalf..."

"My question is *why?* Why is he doing this to me? And why now? It's been over a month, and he has to know my career was trampled over the breakup post he made."

"If I had to take a guess into the frightening mind of a narcissist like Tommy, I'd say it came down to ego. You rejected his advances, and that likely hasn't happened much before. Now, he can't get over it. So, he's rejecting you over and over."

I put my hand to my forehead, feeling like I might faint. "What was the caption?"

"Does it really matter?" I heard papers scrambling on the other end of the line. I'd noticed Janie did that when she was nervous.

"I'd like to know, Janie. Tell me, please. As my friend." She paused and then agreed.

"Okay. He said..." A clicking of the mouse on her computer was heard, then a few punched keys. "*When people say one thing publicly and another privately... God sees it all.*"

"God? He's bringing God into this?" If I didn't blackout before, I must have looked severely at risk, as Tonya walked over to me and put her arm around me. A glance back to the crew told me they saw the photo, too, as all of them were on their phones.

"And your name is trending, attached to this photo. I'm sorry, Sadie. Want to release a statement? Our firm publicist has an incredible way of spinning things and..."

"It's his word against mine. No one would believe me anyway." I felt defeated. Lied about. Slandered. Tommy had implied that we had physical intimacy when we did no such thing. All I ever did was kiss him, in public places, at that. Every kiss we ever shared was probably photographed. The thought made me ill. If I could have taken back every kiss, I would have.

If I could have taken everything back, I'd do it in a heartbeat. I regretted the day I ever met Tommy.

"Sadie, I'm not too good at speaking about Christ, being a new Christian and all but... God knows the truth. And the truth will prevail. I really feel like justice will be served."

"For not being good at it, you sure made me feel better just now." I meant every word. "Thank you, Janie. I better get going."

"Take care, Sadie. Call me any time. I am your friend, too."

"I know. Bye, Janie." We hung up the call, and I gave the phone back to Tonya. She looked deep into my eyes, telling me she knew.

"Someone went after my reputation once," she whispered, as we stood by one of the old western buildings that they made for the set. Judging by the bottles in the window, this one must have been the apothecary. When I didn't respond, she continued. "They said I cheated my way through school. That I didn't deserve the grades I got. That I didn't deserve the career I earned." Pain was in her voice. "The rumors became so widespread that they started calling me Cheat Sheet Tonya. 'At one point, even a teacher slipped and referred to me as that. I thought my life was over."

"I'm sorry to hear that. A teacher? Geez. That's rough." She nodded.

"It was. But it all came to pass when I got a 34 on my ACT. You can't cheat your way through a proctored test that has more security than an airport."

"What happened after that?" I asked. She sighed.

"In a word? Nothing." My eyes widened. "No apologies. No retracted statements. It all just stopped. I moved onto bigger and better things. I got a full-ride scholarship to film school. And now, I'm here, talking to one of the biggest up-and-coming Hollywood stars this generation has ever seen."

"That's all amazing, Tonya. I'd hate to play against you in Jeopardy, but you are wrong about that last part. I've been cancelled by Hollywood." She shook her head.

"I'm going to let you in on a secret." She lowered her voice and looked around. "This movie is indie now, but we have a major producer looking to bump it up. Now, don't get upset if it doesn't happen. But it has everything to do with you, my dear. They want you front and center on the movie poster, in the

promos, in the trailer. That's the catch. We agreed, of course."
My heart skipped a beat.

"No matter what happens, I just want you to know I'm grateful to be here. I love acting. I'd do it for free. And you've blessed me with this project," I said, my earlier tears starting to well up again. Tonya hugged me.

"Don't thank me, darling. You earned your spot in this movie. Now, let's cut for the day. We will finish up the scenes with the guys and get a fresh start tomorrow. Does that sound okay?" I nodded, relieved I could go change out of these clothes and take a long hot bath.

"Thank you, Tonya."

"You're welcome. Please come to me with any issues, okay? Anything. I mean it." I nodded.

"Is this a good time to tell you that this special riding skirt gives me the world's worst wedgie?" Tonya's eyes grew wide before letting out a deep laugh.

"Billy? Where's Rhett?" Tonya's attention went to Billy, who had three horses in tow, guiding them by their lead ropes. Billy shook his head.

"Penny, his horse that he's had since she was just a filly, is missing. He's out looking for her. So, you get me." He smiled, and I could feel Tonya's disappointment. My heart raced thinking I needed to help find Penny, and that's what I did.

*****

Walking a few dozen yards behind Rhett gave me time to think. I knew I'd catch up to him eventually, but I couldn't get my mind off of Tommy's caption. "When people say one thing publicly and another privately... God sees it all." He is implying that I am lying about something. My purity, perhaps? That's something I'd made several public statements about in the teen magazines that had interviewed me. That, and posting that photo... It checked out. My feelings ranged from betrayal, hurt, sadness. But all of these things were outweighed by the need to pray for Tommy. He was so in the wrong, but he thought he was right. He believed he had a relationship with Christ, and then he did things like this. We all make mistakes. We all fall short. But this malicious behavior was concerning me for his soul.

Up ahead, Rhett paused, and I called out his name. At first, he looked up like he didn't know where the voice was coming from. Finally, I was walking with him side by side. We didn't say much until after he said he was losing it. Billy had mentioned Penny had been with Rhett since she was just a baby horse. I could only imagine the feelings going through Rhett's heart right now. It was crucial we found her as soon as possible.

Then, the words started flowing. I asked him about his life, and every time he asked me about mine, I reflected it with the need for knowledge about Wyoming. I had only been here two afternoons, and already my feet couldn't imagine walking on any other soil. My heart couldn't imagine being away from here.

As we walked and talked, a gust of wind picked up.

"This is going to sound weird," Rhett said, stopping in his tracks, as he felt the wind. "But I think I can smell her," he said.

"You can smell her?" I couldn't hold back a smile.

"Don't laugh. It's just something I've always had a keen sense of. I can hear, see, and smell things from a mile away." And here I stood, wondering if I remembered to put on deodorant this morning. If I didn't, and I'd been out walking in this heat and heavy clothing, he would certainly smell me a mile away.

"So, where do you, uh, smell her?"

"I can smell a horse in this direction," he said, as another gust of wind came up. This time, it was more powerful, and nearly knocked me over, blowing my hair completely back.

"What was that?" I said, catching myself before toppling. The sky started darkening, as the wind died down.

"It looks like a storm is about to blow through here. We better take cover," he said, taking me by the arm as we changed directions. In the distance, a dilapidated barn that looked like a big, bad wolf could blow it down with one breath, stood. *Though, 'stood' is a very generous term.*

We both started to run, with him almost pulling me behind him. "Is *that* even considered shelter?" My voice was high strung as we frantically ran towards a structure that looked like it had more risk of falling in on us, than protecting us. Fat, heavy rain drops started falling, slamming into the scalp of my head and my arms. Suddenly, I realized why we were urgently running towards this rather than risking it out here. We may have been swept away by the incoming rain if we didn't.

As we reached the wooden shack, not surprisingly, it didn't cover us from the rain very well. We were both breathless. The sky opened, and the rain fell in buckets. Water was coming in from every point of the roof. Lightning cracked, illuminating purple streaks in the sky for miles. We could see it through a large missing piece just above us. Suddenly, my mind was full of intrusive thoughts of getting struck by lightning right through this gaping roof.

"There's one spot over here that still has a good roof," Rhett said, motioning for me to walk into a muck stall, and I wasted no time walking in. The barn was relatively clean, and considering it got washed out with every rainstorm, I wasn't surprised by this.

As we stood in the stall, rain poured in around us. Thunder clapped in the distance, getting closer and closer. I started to get scared.

"Are we... safe here?" My teeth were chattering as I spoke. Goosebumps covered my arms in the outfit I was just overheating in this afternoon, which now felt like not enough protection from the elements. Rhett instantly removed his jacket and put it around my shoulders.

"We will be safe here, under this roof. You are safe with me." The words stood still between us as every muscle in my body wanted to cling to him. We stood there for moments, minutes— the time was frozen. The sky above was unleashing its thrashing all around us. After a huge boom of thunder, Rhett spoke. "Prayers are always welcome, though." He smiled, trying to lighten the mood. It worked, and I did what he said.

"Dear Jesus, please protect us from this storm. May you keep us out of harm's way by holding up the roof with your hands, Lord. And please protect Penny, for she is wandering out here alone. In Your name, Amen."

"Amen," Rhett said, and I looked up to find his hands clasped together like mine.

"That should do it," I smiled. "But I do feel the Lord's peace now. Do you?" Thunder clapped right above us, and I felt fear again, before having the peace again.

"I do. Thank you, Sadie." While we waited out the storm, a large piece of the roof collapsed in the center of the barn, causing me to scream. Rhett flinched, while I jumped closer to him. His words about being safe with him rang through my mind. Suddenly, my arms were on his chest, as I held onto him for dear life. *A chest that felt like it was chiseled from stone.*

The wind started roaring. Back in California we got the Santa Ana winds, but this was at least ten times that. The sound alone was terrifying. More pieces of the roof fell. Water was coming down in sheets, creeping closer to our feet by the second. As the winds intensified, the water started blowing in at an angle. I clung to Rhett with my arms and Jesus with my heart and mind. Rhett's arms were still stuck to his side, but his stature softened, as if he was trying to be as respectful as possible but allowing me to hold onto him like I might blow away.

For a moment, when nearly all of the roof was coming down, I considered that I may die in this storm. I looked up at Rhett, whose chin came to the top of my head. He had maybe six inches on my height, as I was wearing Pat's cowgirl boots that gave me a lift. I considered that if I was about to meet Jesus, I wanted to look at Rhett one more time. Admire a fine specimen that the Lord made, and all that.

Rhett looked at me, too. Our faces were just inches away from each other. I was hanging onto him with the grip of that baby monkey on his handler in Japan. As we looked into each other's eyes, I lost track of all of my surroundings. The storm could have stopped, and I wouldn't have noticed. Rhett leaned in, just a little closer. I could easily fill the gap and touch my lips to his. I had a feeling that his kiss would be electric. Life altering. Something I would never forget. But then I remembered the phone call I took just before coming out here, and the moment passed as I was filled with defeat. I pulled away from his face, loosening my grip on his chest.

"I'm sorry," Rhett offered instantly, assuming it was his fault.

"No, don't apologize. I'm just... In my head, that's all." It was a little deeper than that, but the trauma in this season of my life just wouldn't go away. "This is moving a little fast, is all. And after the last month..." I trailed off, with the certainty of souring the mood. I wanted to kiss this handsome cowboy, but after kissing Tommy Wheeler, and having that come back to bite me over and over, I didn't know if I should ever kiss anyone ever again. At least not until I knew them far more than I knew Tommy, and I wasn't there yet with Rhett. I shouldn't be kissing people willy nilly.

The storm rattled, but the thunderous booms started sounding further away.

"It's weakening. This has almost passed," Rhett said, his body standing firmer, and I could have sworn I felt him flex his muscles. But the pieces of the roof above us didn't waver. The wood didn't flinch, or bob, or groan with the rest of the pieces. God was protecting us. Rhett was still standing. I was still standing. We weathered this storm. The sky started to clear, with sunshine poking out from behind the dark clouds.

"Thank you, Jesus!" I exclaimed, pulling away from Rhett and putting my hands in the air in praise. God got me through this storm. He would also get me through this storm I was weathering in my personal life.

"He is faithful," Rhett said, readjusting his hat as he assessed the damage around us. "I think we can get out through there." He pointed to a pathway in the barn that wasn't stacked high with old barn wood covered in rusty nails. An opening in the back of the barn wall served as a doorway.

"I don't think this is up to code." I motioned to the fact that the wall had a beam hanging down from it, swinging like a pendulum.

"This place is going to fall down any minute. We need to run out of here. Are you ready?" He held out his hand to me, and I put mine in his, nodding, though I was nervous. It really did look like it was about to collapse.

"I don't know if I can do it," I squeaked, the fear getting the better of me. I started reciting Psalm 23 on repeat. That always worked for me growing up. But instead of pulling me with him, Rhett, in one fluid movement, let go of my hand. He swung one arm around my back, and the other under my knees. Rhett made a run for it, carrying me, just as a beam fell behind him, and I couldn't help but cry out as it scared me.

"Rhett," I screamed, as another beam looked like it was going to fall right on us, but he picked up his speed, navigating through the structure. I closed my eyes as hard as I could, as if that would make this feel less real. I had no idea escaping the barn would feel more dangerous than standing inside of it, but here we were. Finally, the air felt warmer. The sun was touching my skin. I opened up my eyes that had been clenched harder than my butt and jaw put together, and we were outside. We made it. Rhett stood, still holding me, as the barn crumbled down—every last piece, turning it into a heap of sticks, like an Indiana Jones movie.

"Firewood, anyone?" Rhett asked rhetorically, and I let out a deep laugh. He set me down, and I felt a little wobbly on my feet, and I pulled his jacket around me. I didn't need it out here, but it gave me comfort like a weighted blanket. A comfort I wasn't ready to give up just yet.

CHAPTER 16

Rhett

I've never prayed so hard in my life. Except for maybe that one time that I was with my Eagle Scout troop, and we had to traverse several miles across the flats, and it was mud season. I had just learned about quicksand in school, a topic that was so blown out of proportion, I was starting to think it was only told to us in order to sell the major Hollywood movies at the time. But every time I took a step, and my body sunk even an inch into the sticky, wet mess, my heart sank. I wasn't ready to go, not like that. I prayed that whole day that I wouldn't meet my demise in the mud. Today, even in my greater years, I didn't think I could ever top that day.

When the storm came in, we just happened to have this dilapidated shack in sight. This place had been threatening to collapse for years, and yet, it kept standing. What were the odds that the second someone needed it to provide some sort of shelter, it finally would give in? It was a chance I was willing to take. For Sadie's sake. Heck, I could have weathered the storm even out in it. I would have just let the rain hit me. Let the water fill up in my boots. Let the heavens wash all of the dirt and grime of the day away.

Once we were inside the barn, the signs that this wasn't just a regular, run of the mill summer shower were in place. Specifically, the deep, dark rumblings that sounded like it was from the underbelly of the Earth. The wayward lightning that was striking halfway across the sky. The large, heavy raindrops that stung your body as they hit.

As the roof started to come down, my faith peaked. I prayed with every being of my body that Sadie would be spared. I would shield her, protect her from harm's way. *Let the beams fall on me, Lord, not Sadie.* And as she held onto me out of fear and desperation, I felt something familiar. This was the first time we really touched, so I couldn't exactly say what it was. Maybe it wasn't that it was familiar, but that it felt right. Like God was speaking directly to me when her hands touched my chest. At that moment, my heartbeat aligned with hers. I wanted to hold her as close as I could, but I also didn't want to cross any boundaries. The heat of the moment was real. Here she was, a beautiful, enigmatic woman clinging to me like I was the last life preserver at a water park, and I caught myself enjoying every minute of it through my prayers to keep her safe. While asking God to shield her from harm, I was hoping the storm would never end.

As she clung to me, there was a moment when I felt... Anything was possible. I could have sworn that we were about to kiss. A kiss I didn't feel worthy of, for a beauty like Sadie. But her face was right there. Every cell in my brain was flashing the green light, as she looked up at me. I moved my face down just a little ways and... She pulled back. The moment was gone. I thought I had misread the signals, but then again, she looked like she had a hundred different emotions on her face. Sadie still clung to me, saying she was in her head. Implying things about what happened with that slimy ex-boyfriend of hers. My mind went back to the things I saw online about her. She had been through things I would never understand, and the court of public opinion was not kind to Sadie. If anything, she clung to me harder after our near kiss, which was just as good. I continued to pray.

The storm raged on, tearing everything down around us, but we remained. The sliver of roof above us was the only thing that didn't collapse. All glory to God. When it finally did die down, there wasn't much of a pathway to leave. Plus, the boards fallen all over the ground had rusty nails sticking up from every which way. I couldn't risk Sadie stepping on one of them. She was hesitant to walk out, fearing something would fall, as she started to recite some Bible verses. I felt the Holy Spirit take action in my limbs, and I did the only thing I could think to do, and that was carry her out of the disaster zone.

Then the beam came loose. The second we stepped out of the rickety, heap of future firewood, the whole outfit fell to the ground. I held Sadie for another second, perhaps, one second too long, before setting her back down as she struggled to get her bearings. Small tears were welled at the corner of her eyes. Our bodies had been touching for the last several minutes, and now as I stood without her embrace, I wanted to bridge that gap between us. Touching Sadie was like playing with fire; I was feeling the heat, and I was trying to not get too close. I didn't want to get burned. She was leaving here, after all. This was just a temporary stop in her career. But the warmth from the fire was comforting, and I was lost as I watched the enigmatic flames dance before me.

"Here," I said. Reaching into my jeans pocket, I pulled out a strawberry candy. Something I normally only did to reward the little kids that I helped with horseback riding. Sadie was a grown woman, but she had shown just as much bravery as the kids that I got on horses. So, she deserved candy, too.

The sight of the bright, red wrapper made her smile and close her eyes, letting out a small laugh. She took it, carefully unwrapping it and popping it into her mouth. The perfect mouth that I almost just kissed... I swatted the memory away in my mind. As I thought about it, I relished in the fact that God had the perfect plan for my life, even if kissing Sadie at this very moment was all my body wanted. I needed to cool it. Put the brakes on. Let God lead.

"Look!" Sadie yelled, pointing behind me. I turned and saw the most amazing sight: Penny, ambling towards me, like she was just returned from a side quest directed by garden gnomes.

"Penny," I called out, hands on my waist, trying to look stern so she knew she gave me quite the fright. But seeing her just made me praise God even more. He didn't just protect Sadie and me from danger during the storm, but Penny, too.

"Where do you think she was?" Sadie asked.

"It's anyone's guess," I said, as Penny reached us and I put out my hand to pet her neck. "You gave us quite the fright, girl." I turned back to Sadie. "She's still got her saddle and lead on, if you'd like to ride her back? It's quite a long walk to get to the ranch again." A warm breeze picked up as I spoke. Just like that, the cold of the storm had passed, too. A nice, warm summer evening was ahead.

"Is there more candy involved if I do?" Sadie asked with crossed arms.

"Lucky for you, I have an entire bag of these candies back at the ranch, just waiting for signs of bravery." She nodded, and I led Penny a few steps over towards the heap of wood that was a barn. I reached down and put together some stacks of wood that Sadie could use for a step. It took her several minutes to get into the saddle, but I was in no rush. I welcomed the delay, the hesitation, the nervousness from her, as it meant we had more time out here alone. Without the noise and chatter of the ranch, the movie set, or from my family.

Once she was finally in the saddle, the stirrups lined up perfectly to her feet, and she was comfortable with everything, I started walking alongside Penny, who was carrying precious cargo.

"I didn't do anything, you know." I looked up at Sadie, confused.

"What do you mean?" I asked, but she went silent. So, I didn't press. I could feel she had something bubbling up inside of her. Something that wasn't mine to know, but that she needed to get off of her chest. I wondered if her life was as lonely as mine, a thought that surprised me to even consider. I was satisfied with everything that God gave me. But now, knowing Sadie... the pang for more was real. Finally, she spoke up again.

"With Tommy." I nodded. I saw the kiss seen across the world. Everything this woman had done in the last few years had been splashed across the internet for all to see. My heart hurt for her and seeing Tommy on television made it very hard for me to keep true to what Jesus asked of me. I wasn't supposed to hate anyone. I was supposed to love my enemies. Something about Tommy and well.. let's just say, I was praying over my feelings. "No one believes me, but I made a commitment to

Christ for purity until marriage and that is very much still a thing."

"I believe you," was all I could muster. None of this was my business, but I wanted her to know I cared for her. Believing her was the least I could do.

"Thanks," she said, flatly. "Now, he's saying... he's implying that..." Suddenly, she was crying. The second fountain of water that I wasn't expecting today. Penny stopped, as I did, and I waited. I wanted to comfort her. "He's making it seem like we did things. And the world thinks I just threw my purity away on a guy that I knew for what, a month?" The tears continued.

"It's going to be okay," I said, my hand reaching for hers, and I held it. My hand started sweating like I was in elementary school. "Just like the storm we just had... this, too, shall pass. I mean it, Sadie. Only God can judge us, and the minds of Hollywood are not always in line with the sight of Heaven. Those people can have their priorities majorly out-of-whack. Just take this for instance: A beautiful woman, with a great future ahead of her, dates a pretend cowboy who's now trying to ruin her reputation, and everyone takes his side?" The words slipped out before I meant them too. Not only did I let on that I knew the situation she was in, but it must have seemed that I, too, had been caught reading up on all of her personal drama. Her cheeks reddened and her tears started to dry up. She gave me a little nod.

"Thank you," she whispered, and standing there, I waited for more. For more to hear, for more to say. But she didn't say anything at all, so I started walking again, with Penny in stride with me, step by step.

"You know what time it is?" I asked, looking at the sky as I walked.

"What?" She sounded like the question was the most intriguing thing she'd ever heard.

"It's almost dinner time. We've been out here for hours, you know. I feel like I could eat like a bear."

"The kind of bear that roots through garbage cans?" she asked with a giggle.

"Exactly. We don't have many trash pandas out here, but we still get a few. Ever since the guy that lives a few miles north from here started raising them as pets—heck, we have even less. I think they've just been biding their time, hoping to be domesticated. Begging him to take them in. They wanted off the streets." The thought of seeing one of our neighbors, Earl, at the hardware store with a baby raccoon sitting on his truck dashboard made me chuckle.

"Wait—did you mean your neighbor is raising raccoons? Like, as in, animals with rabies?" I nodded.

"Apparently, if you raise them from cubs, it's totally okay."

"What is he—a raccoon-ologist? Who says it's okay?" She laughed and scrunched her nose. The more I thought about my goofy neighbor, who seemed smarter than most but also painfully introverted, I shrugged my shoulders.

"He just may be a raccoon scientist or whatever you just said." We both laughed now, cackling at the idea of the cute little critters running around his house.

"I think I'd like to see this raccoon farm," she whispered. "Do they allow visitors?" I shrugged my shoulders.

"I haven't checked the admission prices in a while," I teased. "But I bet if we gave him a call, he'd be happy to bring a few over for you to meet."

"I think I'd like that." Sadie laughed again, the darkness of the earlier conversation lifted.

"Great. He will be happy to meet you. He loves showing off those little things. Last year, they were in the live nativity at church."

"Raccoons in the nativity?" She asked with disbelief.

"We had donkeys, a few cows and yeah, little Johnny the raccoon was in there too."

"You are just now telling me they have names?" She was gasping for breath with laughter.

"Of course they have names. Let's see: other than Johnny I've met Linda, Patricia and Carl. You will really win them over if you bring them treats."

"All this food talk—I think I've worked up an appetite."

"Don't worry. Just a few more miles ahead, there's a dumpster."

CHAPTER 17

Sadie

It was an emotionally charged afternoon. Rhett's words hit me like an arrow to the heart. Telling me that he believed me? Turned out, that was just what I needed to hear. That someone believed me. It gave me comfort that God was still working through this situation. Rhett was right—this too shall pass. It didn't matter what others thought because God knew the truth. I just wished this trial didn't hit me on such a personal level.

Implying that I'd given up my purity, which was a commitment I made to the Lord to wait until I was married, made me feel all sorts of things towards Tommy. Anger. Sadness. A few fleeting feelings of blinding rage. But after the long ride back, miles I didn't even remember walking earlier to find the very horse I was now sitting on, God gave me the clarity I needed.

I didn't hate Tommy. I felt sorry for him. He was so far from a true, meaningful relationship with Christ that I didn't even realize it until he did all of these things. It was a good reminder that even though someone says they are in Christ—professing it with their mouths and in his case, all over his social media—it may not be true. In this case, it was his actions that really made me wonder. I didn't need to hate Tommy. God had promised that He would take revenge. He would fight our battles. The only thing I needed to do? I needed to pray for Tommy.

Then, Rhett said I was beautiful. Yes, I'd heard this before, from movie executives. From fans. From comments on my social media. From potential agents, before I found Janie, which was why working with a woman felt better for me. More comfortable. But hearing it from Rhett's mouth, a man so ruggedly handsome that he was the epitome of masculinity, made me weak in the knees. If I hadn't been sitting on Penny, I would have nearly fainted.

"Thank you," was all I could muster out at the time. The words fell short of how he made me feel today, though. I wasn't just falling for his words. I was falling for his actions. How he protected me in the barn. How he carried me to safety. How he made sure I was okay. He made me feel like I was a woman who deserved all of these things. Like I wasn't just a disposable actress that, when cancelled, would be replaced by a dozen more young blondes waiting for their chance at dating Tommy Wheeler. Rhett made me feel like I hadn't felt in years: like a normal person.

The whirlwind of the day was coming down on me hard as we made it back to the ranch. Rhett, quick on his feet, led Penny to the corral where he grabbed the portable stairs and ran them over to me. I felt stiff and for a moment, couldn't remember how to get off the horse.

"Just take your time, Sadie. Put all of your weight in one stirrup and swing the other leg over. Hold onto the saddle horn." Both of my legs felt like they were carrying all of the weight, and it took a few tries for me to get out of the saddle, but I finally did.

"I guess this was our lesson for the day, then?" I asked, remembering yesterday that we were supposed to have a lesson where we left the corral. The one I had called a *date.* Having been out with him now, it felt so much more intimate than a date ever could. He reached into his pocket and handed me one more candy.

"I suppose so," he said, smiling. A sight that I'd only seen in short glances. A sight that felt as powerful as sunlight kissing my face. "Unless you're up for one right now? Penny still has some gas in her tank. I can wrangle up my pack horse, and we can head straight for the mountains, not stopping until we make it to the ridge line." The eagerness in his voice made me wonder if he was actually joking or not. Then, he winked. And if I wasn't feeling faint before, I was now. I held onto the corral gates behind me for strength. I didn't think he noticed, but then again, this was the type of man who noticed everything in the best way. The type of man that I wanted to be around. The type of man that I wanted to marry one day... The thought about knocked me down. That was my cue. It was time to walk away.

"I'll see you at dinner," I said, as I forced myself to walk to my cabin. But before I did, I heard a familiar sound. A snap. A camera lens shuttered. I found myself standing a little straighter. Feeling sobered from this witty flirtation happening with zero abandon as I stood next to the hunkiest (real) cowboy I'd ever laid eyes on. "Did you hear that?" I whispered, and he took another step towards me, looking out into the prairie.

"I heard it," he whispered back. As we looked all around us, there was a slight movement out by the riverbanks. My heart started pounding. Was there a paparazzi here that just took photos of me standing close to Rhett? Was I about to be splashed in the tabloids again for something considered indecent, taken out of context? We weren't even touching. Sure, the sparks were flying, but it made me second guess all of it now, knowing that it might soon see the light of day to the rest of the world.

After a moment, Rhett's brother Wyatt and darling daughter, Gracie, emerged from the riverbank, carrying two fishing poles. He was holding Gracie's hand, and when he looked up and saw us staring at him, he looked behind him instinctively.

"You look like you've seen a ghost, a grizzly bear, or that raccoon Tammy wearing her favorite pink sweater," Wyatt quipped. Rhett crossed his arms.

"What's up, Wyatt?" Rhett looked serious. I was very concerned that there was more to this story. But Wyatt just shrugged.

"Just a little fishing. Didn't catch anything, but I got some cute action shots to send to mom." He pulled out his phone and showed us the photo of Gracie trying to reel in her line that was ultimately caught on a stick. I let out a breath of relief. There was no paparazzi—just Wyatt. Rhett seemed to soften at this, too. All I could think of when the exchange came to an end was that I did not have the advantage of flirting with someone I thought was handsome without the world knowing about it. I did not have the advantage of keeping my private life private. If you were a celebrity, people thought that your life was their open book to read whenever they wanted. They thought they knew you. That they deserved to have all of the facts. Honestly, being out here in Wyoming and spending time away from the glamour of it all... I wasn't sure it was the life I really wanted to lead.

"I'll see you all later," I said to Rhett, Wyatt, and Gracie, giving Gracie a pat on the head. They all said their goodbyes, while Rhett looked particularly regretful of my leaving.

Walking back to my cabin, I knew things were changing for me. I was already contemplating if I ever wanted to leave. Sure, I loved acting. Living out a scene, playing a character that was different—what was entertainment for others was for me, as well. But the path I was on—er, what I thought I was on, before Tommy Wheeler dumped me, and everyone took his side—was that the place I really wanted to be?

In the cabin, there was a fresh bouquet of flowers sitting on the table with ample sprigs of lavender all around, filling up my senses. Pat must have been here. Laid out on the bed, I had a freshly laundered set of clothes set out to change into after my hot bath. A fresh, fuzzy bathrobe was slung over the door to the tub. As I drew a hot bath, pouring an ample amount of fragrant bubbles into the basin, I thanked God for such a simple pleasure in life.

After a relaxing bath, I called and checked in with my parents. They were thrilled to hear all about Wyoming and were very interested in my retelling of the horseback riding scenes.

"It sounds like you're on the adventure of a lifetime, dear," my mom said, sweetly.

It was not Australia, but to speak the truth, I wasn't much of a fan of deep water anyway. The thought of filming the ocean scenes in the shark movie was riddling me with anxiety. Yes, I did much prefer the old west and the open prairie to sharks. Whether they had teeth or not, I found the idea frightening.

After I hung up with my parents, I checked my very full inbox of emails. Nothing that couldn't be put off, I thought, so I went to my texts and opened a message to send one to my best friend, Molly.

Me: I have really survived something today.

Molly: You accidentally joined a square dancing contest and won, and you're now being recruited to join *Dancing with the Stars?*

Me: Well, shoot. Now, no matter what I say, it's not going to sound as fun in comparison.

Molly: So, if it wasn't a dance-off between you and a man named Earl...?

Me: A storm. It was like, biblical.

Molly: Define biblical. Plagues? Locusts? A parting of the sea?

Me: One part dilapidated barn. One part flooding rain. The rest was all scary lightning and thunder that felt like it might kill me at any moment.

Molly: STOP.

Molly: Were you alone???

Me: ...

Molly: I am sitting down.

Me: His horse Penny ran off. We went looking for her. A storm hit. Barn was questionable at best.

Molly: Please tell me that the "his" is RHETT.

Me: ...

Molly: Is it just me, or was this scene ripe for a heroic move from the ole' cowboy?

Me: Well, he did carry me.

Molly: I'M SORRY, WHAT?

Me: The roof was literally falling in.

Molly: Did he say something memorable? Please tell me he did. His online presence seems like he would.

Me: "You're safe with me."

Molly: I need a minute.

Molly: DID YOU KISS HIM?

Me: No.

Molly: Why are you like this?

Me: It didn't feel right.

Molly: Elaborate immediately.

Me: I was in my head. After everything with Tommy... I just couldn't.

Molly: That actually makes sense. I don't want it to make sense. I hate that it makes sense.

Me: Also, I nearly died.

Molly: Details.

Me: The barn collapsed after we ran out.

Molly: Of course it did.

Me: He gave me a strawberry candy.

Molly: I'm sorry, what now?

Me: He rewards bravery with strawberry candy.

Molly: That is the cutest trope I've ever heard of for a main character in this movie.

Me: Except he's not a character. He's a real cowboy. And this is real life.

Molly: You're right. Marry him.

Me: Molly.

Molly: Fine. Court him. With chaperones and church settings.

Me: ...

Molly: What's on the agenda tonight?

Me: Dinner is in a little bit. But I'm so tired, I feel like I could faint.

Molly: Good. You'll sleep well. Go get some nourishment and maybe the cowboy has a few tunes up his sleeve tonight.

Me: I hate that I'm so curious if he is singing tonight.

Molly: There's nothing wrong with liking someone, Sadie.

Me: Maybe there is? Look what happened with Tommy.

Molly: Tommy is a jerk, Sadie. I'm sorry that you didn't see it before. Sure, he's handsome but.. Some men just don't know how to treat a woman with grace and respect. And look how Hollywood has only rewarded him for his behavior...

Me: That's all very true.

Molly: Okay, storm survivor. Go on and find some grub and see if there's music to the wind tonight...

Me: Goodnight, Molly.

CHAPTER 18

Rhett

"Rhett?" My mom, Pat, called from the dining hall. I was heading in there shortly, having triple checked the horse corral for any way that Penny could escape and was satisfied with it.

"Hi." I walked over and gave her a kiss on the cheek.

"I heard about Penny." She motioned with her head towards my prized horse. "What happened?" I shrugged.

"I don't know. Best I can guess is that someone accidentally opened the back of the corral. Don't think any big wind gusts came through that could do it." She nodded.

"Speaking of the storm." A sly smile crossed her face.

"Ever since, you look different." I cocked an eyebrow.

"Did I go prematurely gray today and haven't noticed yet?" My mom shook her head.

"Just something different about you, is all." She shrugged, her smile pasted across her face like she was in on a secret.

"Okay, then," I tried to say casually. But my mom always knew things somehow, and finally I cracked like an egg and smiled back.

"You like her," she said. It wasn't a question.

"It doesn't matter what I like," I said, sorrowfully. "She's leaving here and that's it."

"You don't get to disqualify yourself for her just because she's here on an assignment."

"We're from two different worlds," I said. She let out an earnest laugh.

"That doesn't mean anything. Opposites attract."

"Not when one of the opposites would have to leave here for Hollywood." I could never live under the palm trees in a city so... crowded. I required elbow room. Quiet peace. A vast open prairie where I could ride my horses off in the sunset.

"You always think you have to be in control of everything, my son. You've been like this since you were just a boy. But you don't know what she wants, Rhett. Don't try and decide for her." I shrugged, but I took in what she said. Word for word. The truth stung. I was a control freak. Always had been. But the truth was, with Sadie? I felt... reckless. Out of control. Freedom from myself. And I was starting to loosen the reins on my own heart.

"I just..." I trailed off.

"You don't want to get hurt?" My mom finished my sentence. I nodded, not looking her in the eye, but instead, looking off to the movie set in the near distance. The fake saloon looked pretty cool in the prairie. "My son, I've seen you do this your whole life. If you wanted the same thing as someone else, you would pretend you didn't, just in case they got it instead of you." She paused. "I saw it on your face when Wyatt brought Sophie home," she said, looking right at me. I moved my gaze to hers. She had my full attention now. "You have never spoken up for yourself, son. And that might be admirable for most cases. Take Wyatt and Sophia: They make a wonderful pair. You couldn't live the life they have built together; you have different ideas of home. I'm sure you see that now, but part of me wanted you to figure that out from firsthand experience of dating someone. This fear of getting hurt has to end. Sometimes hurt is the price of loving."

I didn't say anything. Instead, I reached in for a hug. My mom was a great reader of people. She loved everyone around her with all that she had. And she was always right, in every situation.

"Thanks, Mom," I whispered.

"You are worthy of love. And I've seen the way she looks at you, Rhett. I know it's still early but sometimes, we just know."

"We?" I asked. My mom nodded.

"I knew the day I met your father that he was the one. I had just broken up with Bobby Phillips after we courted for ten days. Some teased at the time that I was on the rebound. Truthfully, Bobby was just not right for me in so many ways. I never mourned that breakup. Instead, I felt relieved. My parents took a few days to get on board, as they had been best friends with Bobby's parents, but once they met your father, well... It's safe to say everyone fell in love with him just as quickly as I did."

"Bobby Phillips? As in, the man who owns the hardware store, grocery store, and all the gas stations from here to Nebraska?" I was surprised to hear about this revelation, as she had never shared this with me before.

"All of the money and success in the world doesn't mean a thing if you don't have love." And with that, she walked towards the dining hall. "I better get going. Pasta primavera tonight and my mother's garlic bread recipe." My stomach growled at the news she was making my favorite meal for dinner.

"I can't wait," I said, waving her off.

"I'll make an extra loaf just for you," she said with a laugh, as she disappeared through the dining room door.

*****

After feeding the horses, I went back to my cabin for a shower and shave before dinner. As I lathered up my face to shave, I looked in my reflection in the mirror. I didn't see what my mom was saying; I didn't think I looked any different. But I felt different. My mom was right about many things, per usual. I was falling hard for Sadie. I was letting myself do that. But I wasn't going to believe that Sadie was feeling the same way about me. She could have any man in the world, anywhere in the world. Why on earth would a woman like her, pure grace, beauty, and glamour, pick a guy like me, covered in dirt head to toe in this dustbowl of a state—to love? Surely, she could find some clean-cut man who liked dressing up and doing red carpet events alongside her. The thought of me on a red carpet was laughable. Sure, I had that brown suit that I bought for my brother's wedding. It had leather flaps on the jacket and a bright turquoise bolero. Along with the right boots, I started to think I could almost pull it off, when I smacked myself in the forehead.

"Get a grip, man!" I told myself in the mirror. "Daydreaming about what you'd wear on the red carpet? What is this?" Then suddenly, I saw it: I did look different. There was a lightness to my face. Not in color—I was still as tan as I could get, and my permanent, five o'clock shadow was there, just shorter, the moment I shaved. No... I'd say this was something different entirely. *I looked happy.* And it was quite possible that this fact scared me more than anything.

*****

In the dining room that evening, my eyes immediately scanned the room for Sadie. She was sitting at a table full of her crew, but there was one seat open next to her. As I went to fill my plate at the buffet-style serving setup, I used all of my willpower to not look back at her while I was gathering up food. That would have been ridiculous. Too obvious. But the pain of not looking over my shoulder was growing. I wanted to see her face again. I wanted to see her smile. See if she was laughing. To see if she was getting enough to eat.

Finally, my plate was heavy with my favorite foods, topped off with practically an entire loaf of garlic bread. My mom only made this recipe once a month, and my mouth could water on command just thinking about it any time of the day or night. I was certainly going to eat as much of it as I could when I had the opportunity. As I turned around to assess the room again, I reminded myself I had never sat with any of the guests. No one had. In fact, most of the staff just came and took food back to their living quarters to eat in front of the television or with their friends. It would be pretty bizarre behavior to change that now.

I saw a two-seater table at the back of the room, with my dad sitting alone. Perfect. I walked past everyone, including Sadie, and I felt her eyes on me. I felt the temperature of the room rise. I felt like I'd forgotten how to put one foot in front of the other.

"Hi, Rhett," Sadie called out, and her entire table fell quiet.

"Yes, good evening, Rhett," Tonya called out afterwards. There was a stifled giggle from one of the other crew members, but I didn't see who it was. I turned as casually as I could, but ended up looking really stiff, as if all of the muscles in my neck were pulled.

"H-hey," I said with a nod, looking at both women, but my eyes landed back on Sadie.

"You must really like that bread," Sadie said, acknowledging my plate. I smiled.

"It's my favorite thing to eat," I said back to her, feeling like every word that came out was stiffer than the word before. The crew around Sadie just looked at me as if they were waiting for me to break out into song. "Well, enjoy your meal," I said, as I walked to my dad.

"You must really like that bread," my dad teased, as I sat down across from him. I gave him a playful glare, and he took a big bite out of his own bread. As he chewed, the aroma of garlic all around me, he leaned in and whispered, "If the roles were reversed and that was your mother sitting there at that table full of people with an open seat beside her, you best believe my rear end would be taking it."

"Is it that obvious to everyone?" I asked him. He gave me a slow nod with unwavering eye contact.

"Does the crew know, too?" He just nodded back. Dread filled my stomach. When the Broken Arrow Ranch was approached by this production company, they said that they had several western movies that they wanted to film and if all went well with this one... Well, they could do them here. In my mind, if the production company perceived that their stars were getting hit on by the staff, well... It was just not good for my family's ranch. I needed to straighten up. Things might have been happening in my heart, but for the ranch's sake, I needed to remain professional. That was a heck of a lot easier said than done.

After we finished our meal, I decided I needed some time in prayer to sort out my feelings. Today was a big day. I could skip the campfire. My dad would keep the fire going for our guests, as he usually did when I wasn't there, and the guests didn't need to hear my music tonight. I slipped out of the dining hall without looking back at Sadie.

CHAPTER 19

Sadie

That night, Rhett wasn't at the fire. I had been hoping to see him, and when I made eye contact with Billy, he gave me a smile and shrugged, as if he knew exactly what, or who, I was looking for.

*****

Before I knew it, the days went by like lightning in the sky. The filming schedule was getting more intense by the day; it was clear to me then that the crew had been easing me into things the first few days when I had so much free time. My lessons with Rhett became more about our talks than riding—not that my skills didn't improve dramatically, because they did. As I rode, Rhett was such a distraction that I didn't even realize the speeds I was gaining or how much trust I had given Penny. I also found myself falling harder for Rhett every moment. It wasn't about his looks—they were there—oh, believe me that he was the most stunning creation on earth. But his entire being—his mind, his soul—wrapped up with mine in ways that felt so natural, so right. I had to pinch myself that this was real.

Each day, I'd film for several hours. The horseback riding scenes were getting more challenging, as I was filmed riding around at high speeds often, but surprisingly, I had less and less time booked with Rhett each day. Still, we'd savor the moments together. As I headed into my second full week of filming, I was sad to see that some things were already wrapping up. Some minor cast members were already released to go back to their homes. I was to be leaving soon. But the longer I was in Wyoming, the less I wanted to be anywhere else.

One morning, filming was at sunrise, so most of the crew had breakfast served to them in the field. Pat made everyone large breakfast burritos with all the fixings—eggs, hashbrowns, sausage, mushrooms, onions, and ample amounts of cheese. It sounded great, but my stomach was just not ready that early in the morning to consume copious amounts of calories. So, after we wrapped up the first half of the day, I headed to the dining hall, hoping to find something I could eat for a late breakfast and thankfully, Pat was there.

"Hi, sweetie. I noticed you didn't eat breakfast this morning, so I prepared you this egg white frittata. Extra fruit on the side, and some crispy breakfast potatoes. How does that sound?" My stomach rumbled in reply.

"Are you an angel?" I asked sincerely, as she sat a fresh plate down. "How did you know I was coming just now?" Pat shrugged.

"I have the entire shooting schedule, and I just thought you might." She gave me a little wink as she set the beautiful food down in front of me. Colorful cherry tomatoes, bright green spinach, and even some of those sliced mushrooms made up the frittata. I was so blessed. Saying a prayer over my food, I dug in, feeling the nourishment hit my bones.

"How is everything going with horseback riding?" Pat asked, when I was mid-chew. Did she mean, how are things going with her son? Or, with my skills and abilities riding? I tilted my head and decided the latter was a much safer assumption.

"I feel very confident riding. I don't know if you saw it a few days ago—I had that scene where I chased the wolf out of the town on horseback. Of course, we weren't going that fast, and the wolf will be CGI. But Penny is such a good girl to ride that she made it easy." I lovingly looked over to the corral where beautiful Penny was grazing. I was really becoming a horse person after spending time with her.

"Sounds very exciting! I'm so happy for you, Sadie. Are you working with Rhett today?" Just the sound of his name sent electricity to my joints and a craving for strawberry candy to my brain.

"Yes. I'm meeting him at three. We are going to ride along the river, do some practice runs for the scene where I cross it on horseback. I also have to practice my quick dismounts." My nerves suddenly were on fire. Though I was gaining confidence every day, mostly in Penny's ability to keep me upright, I was still so nervous about riding performatively. Doing things correctly. Looking the part.

"That sounds great, dear. I look forward to hearing how your lesson goes." My ears perked up, and she held her gaze, as if she was begging me to ask why exactly she would hear about it. She offered the bait, and I took it.

"Does Rhett... talk to you... about me?" I stammered the words out, and with each syllable, Pat looked more and more welcoming of my question.

"Oh yes, dear. But it's because I ask him how things go with our guests at the end of every day. Sometimes, I really have to pull it out of him, but sometimes..." She trailed off, spiking my curiosity tenfold. I set down my fork, suddenly wringing my hands together on my lap. Again, my mind was all too aware this behavior was for a man I'd known for all of a week, but my heart didn't care. Rhett was unlike any man I'd ever met, in the best way possible.

"Sometimes?" I finally asked when she didn't elaborate. She returned my question with the biggest smile I had ever seen, letting me know that she had been sizing up my interest this whole time.

"Sometimes, he looks like he's walking on clouds after your time together." My heart skipped a beat. I felt the same way and now, his mom knew it. I knew it. Did Rhett know? The realization that I was leaving here in a matter of two weeks hit me once again. All of this was temporary. I was just setting myself up for heartbreak. Pat sensed something shifted. "What's wrong, dear?" She pulled out the chair in front of me and took a seat. A few crew members had shuffled in the back door, looking for Tonya, and then quickly left again.

"It's just that... I'm leaving here soon. After this movie is complete, I'm heading back to Ohio, which is a long way away from Wyoming." Pat nodded.

"Is that home, then? Here I assumed you lived in California." I shrugged.

"Technically, I do, but I sublet my condo after the whole... You know. I just needed a break and what better rest and relaxation than moving back in with your parents as an adult after living apart from them?" We both laughed. "I mean, I love them so much. But it's hard, too. I'm just so blessed to be spending time out here. There's just something about this ranch... about Wyoming that speaks to my soul in ways I've never heard before. It's going to be really hard to leave." Just then, Rhett walked by the window. His long legs were wearing different jeans today. Jeans that I couldn't help but notice, he wore well. It took everything I had to peel my eyes off of him and look back at his mother, to which she noticed, as I was greeted with her approving smile.

"Our Rhett is a special one. He will never come out and say it to me, but I can tell that boy is falling faster than a calf at a cattle branding." I felt all the skin on my body blush at that very moment. "Oh my. Are you having a hot flash?" Pat stood, retrieving a pitcher of ice water and pouring me a glass. "Or, is this 'hots-for-the-cowboy-itis'?" I nearly choked on my water that I immediately began chugging.

"It may be a little of both," I admitted with a nervous laugh. It was true. Rhett had an effect on me. But sitting here talking about it with his mom was hilarious because not only was she encouraging it, she was hoping we would like each other. At least that's how it seemed.

"I'll let you finish your meal in peace, without a mother's incessant badgering for you to like her son." And with that, she winked and returned to the kitchen where she started preparing lunch. I was stunned. At least I knew I had her blessing.

While I finished my frittata, I considered that Pat would make an excellent mother-in-law. To someone. Someday. Just because she liked me, and I liked her son, a topic that I was slowly accepting more every minute, didn't mean anything would come from this. I was here on business, after all. Fighting for a career that was nearly taken from me because of one man's words. Just as I finished my food, Tonya came walking in the dining room.

"Just the girl I was looking for," she said with a half-smile.

"I actually think they are looking for you." The look on her face told me she already knew that people were trying to track her down.

"Two things: First, we had to bump your horseback riding lesson for today. We have to reshoot the last scene again, as the lighting was a little off, and Ben's makeup was all wrong." The disappointment was palpable. "Secondly, Janie sent a message to me this morning, and that message is here on this phone." Tonya held a phone in front of her, but her body language told me she wasn't ready for me to see it yet. I went back to my fruit plate.

"Let me guess: Tommy said that I'm still secretly pining for him and won't leave him alone?" I just said the most ridiculous thing I could imagine, followed by a laugh. Tonya fell silent. I turned to her, very slowly, as if any sudden movements would make this nightmare a reality. "Tonya? That's not what happened, is it?" She looked down regretfully.

"I'm sorry, Sadie. Do you want to see the post?" If my eyes got any wider, surely my eyeballs would fall out onto the floor like in a cartoon. My hands shook as she handed me the cell phone. I was face to face with a post on Tommy Wheeler's social media account.

Another photo of Tommy standing next to me, splashed across his profile. Questions tumbled through my mind. This picture was taken at the awards show, before the fateful kiss seen around the world. The cameraman was doing most of the work at the angles in this. There I was, Tommy's arm around me. He was looking straight ahead, and I was looking at him like he was the treasure I'd been searching for my entire life. I looked delusionally obsessed with him. And, on my left hand, the gorgeous rock from the Rodeo Drive jeweler on full display. The caption? Icing on the cake.

"Some people are in a rush for a ring. I'm not." Another blow to my image. But why was he doing this? Then, I remembered that moment. I wasn't looking at Tommy. I was looking *past* Tommy, at the catering cart that just wheeled out several dozen treats for attendees to snack on. My look was love, desire, and intensity—for dessert, not Tommy.

"Tonya... This is so out of context." She nodded.

"I figured as much. Your agent, Janie, asked me to consult with you about it. I'm sort of the liaison in charge of this now. What would you like me to do? Anything?" Sure, there was plenty I wanted to say. To yell from the mountain tops that Tommy Wheeler was a liar about all of it. But the more I'd thought about it the last few weeks, the more I wanted to keep my mouth shut. God knew what happened. The people I cared for knew what happened. For those who wanted to believe someone lying, nothing I said would change their minds. It would only be spun to make me look more desperate, weaker, and petty.

"Nothing for now. Thank you for bringing this to my attention," I said, God filling my heart with the peace that only He could provide. "I do have one request though," I said, my voice feeling stronger.

"Anything," Tonya pleaded, holding her phone out as if she was ready to type up a statement. A comeback. Revenge of any kind.

"It's clear that Tommy is... going through something. I don't understand why he's targeting me with these lies, but that is all that they are." Tonya nodded, lapping up the words. "But may I ask that, whatever else comes up, you don't tell me?" Her jaw dropped. "It's just that... I don't want to hate him. I want to continue praying for him. He's very lost and... seeing these posts makes that harder, sure... but I don't want to stoop to his level." Tonya, holding her phone like a cross on her chest, looked like she was trying to understand.

"But, people need to know that he's a liar. He's literally running all around the internet implying things that can ruin your reputation!" Her words inflamed my cheeks again. Pat shuffled out from the kitchen, carrying a pitcher of lemonade that was loaded with fresh sprigs of lavender. As she placed the pitcher next to my plate of food and filled a glass, I remembered what Rhett had told me, about God knowing the truth.

"It doesn't matter if he's lying about me," I said, the words surprising even myself, as I felt the Holy Spirit was over me. "God knows the truth, and the truth will prevail. Maybe not right now. Maybe not in my lifetime. But His will is greater than these lies, and no matter what, He is still writing the script for me, not Tommy. Let him lie. Let him imply. I will live by my faith and my actions alone." Tonya's jaw nearly touched the floor of the dining room, as she nodded.

"Thanks, Sadie. I will, uh, pass that along to Janie." Tonya spun around and left the room as fast as she had entered.

"Well done, dear," Pat said, giving my arm a squeeze. I let out a breath.

"I'm sorry you had to hear that," I said, woefully. My hands were a little shaky and my stomach was in turmoil. I reached for the glass of lavender lemonade and downed half of it before I even tasted the glorious sweetness.

"I'm sorry I interrupted. I hope you don't think I'm one of those nosy eavesdroppers. But, I'm glad I could hear it. It's not every day that you get to be a witness to someone taking the high road in such a fallen world."

As we chatted for a few more minutes, I thanked her for the wonderful meal and headed back to my cabin for some solitude, reflection, and prayer. Standing up to the drama wasn't easy for me and anytime I was firm with someone, I felt like I was being confrontational. This time was no exception.

CHAPTER 20

Rhett

I hadn't had much time with Sadie in the last week. Today, we were supposed to have a good hour to ride together, but that was cancelled. Every day, we had less of a lesson and more of a bonding time, as her skills had improved so much. Sure, I'd been milking out the time where I could, trying to show her new things, but Sadie was a natural on a horse. If this were the 1800's, like in her movie, she would have made an excellent pioneer woman. So much so, that I found myself praying at night for God to turn back time. Wake me up in a moment where we were living in the old west. Where Sadie could belong here, with me, in Wyoming.

Despite my feelings that I did feel were reciprocated, and her love for earning the pieces of strawberry candy at the end of the lessons, our time was wrapping up. I knew I was in my head about it. Like my mom said, I didn't get to decide what other people wanted. I didn't get to decide what other people did. But the only thing I could control was myself. And right now, it couldn't have been more clear to me that Sadie was just going to leave here and take my heart with her. Life on this ranch, the place I loved more than anywhere on earth, despite my lack of travel through it, would never be the same. And, if one day I did find someone to marry, I didn't want to still be holding a candle for a woman I knew over a three-week period while she was filming on location. That wouldn't be fair to my future wife. That wouldn't be right in my walk with the Lord.

So, I decided then that I would be honest with Sadie. I knew what I was going to say. I just needed the right time to do it. But when I woke up this morning, I realized I didn't get any time with her the next few days. Not even a moment where we practiced her riding. Her dismounts. Her slowing down Penny once she worked up a good trot. Not that Sadie needed much more of that. Like I said, her moves were natural. I'd never seen anything like it. It was as if Penny and her spoke the same language.

When I saw Sadie leaving the dining hall, likely headed for her cabin, I knew I had to take the chance. I hoped and prayed she would linger for a moment so I could get these things off my chest. When she did, I felt like the luckiest man in the world. Things started off on the right track. "Going swimmingly," as my dad always said. But then, I felt things sour. My mind took over my heart. I no longer let it be a mutual decision, and I feared I ruined things altogether. As it was happening, it was like I was watching it unfold, but I couldn't stop the words from coming out of my mouth. I couldn't hit the brakes on this fast moving train; it had already left the station.

CHAPTER 21

Sadie

As I walked back to my cabin, Rhett was standing in the horse corral. I locked eyes with him. The physical attraction I felt to this cowboy was unlike anything I'd ever felt. My entire being wanted to wrap my arms around his neck and kiss him. He took a step forward.

"Hi," I said, the fluster from Tonya far from my mind as I eagerly walked towards him, stopping at the corral gate panels.

"Hey, Hollywood," he said, playfully. A nickname that normally wouldn't make me laugh, as Hollywood and I were not currently on the best terms. But coming from Rhett, it was somehow making me feel special.

"We're on a nickname basis now, huh?" I teased. "Now I need one for you. Let's see: 'Wranglers' is a good place to start,"

I joked, pointing to his obviously brand new jeans. Was he wearing them, or were they wearing him? It was hard to tell at this point. Rhett just smiled, his jawline doing all the work for him as usual.

"I was hoping I would still see you today," he mentioned, my heart skipping all of the next twenty beats.

"I just heard about our time being cancelled." I looked at him with gloom. "I don't think I'm scheduled with you again for a few days." A fact that I found quite disturbing and maybe he did, too. He'd just taken a step towards me again, and my hands squeezed the panels in anticipation. Just the look in his eyes told me he wanted this, too. That he felt the same way I had since the moment I saw him. But then, he stopped short. This time, he was the one ending what could have happened before it did.

"Sadie..." he paused, his voice rich with a hesitation that told me he had practiced this speech in his head. "I want to clear the air." My heart skipped again.

"Okay," was all I could muster.

"I feel something... happening between us." His words rang through my heart like a song. "But"—there went my pulse again, hearing the words that were never welcome—"I don't want to be another headline in your life," he said, in his deep voice that carried through my mind. For a moment, it felt like someone had pulled the air out of my lungs. Here I was, standing in front of a man, who once told me I was beautiful, that just said he felt something happening between us, and now this? My mind started to wander as I fell into a prayer. *Lord, does Rhett think I'm damaged goods? Too much drama? Not worth the risks?* Before I could pray any more, Rhett interrupted my thoughts. "I'm not saying I don't want this." His voice turned into a whisper, and a rush of relief washed over me. "But we hardly know each other, and... I want to take things slow. I don't want my picture splashed all over the internet in another accusation that you've... done something you shouldn't have. I don't want to be the reason that people attack you even more than they already are." I nodded, appreciating the words from this man.

"Thank you, Rhett, for considering me. It's funny you bring this up now, as I've just told Tonya that—". My words stopped short, as I swore I heard another camera lens shutter.

"There are eyes all over this place," Rhett spoke quietly, as I felt instantly sobered from the attraction and stood up straighter, looking around with wide eyes.

"Are there people here that we can't trust?" I whispered, my mind racing to imagine who it could be. Rhett shrugged.

"Everyone who works here is trustworthy. I'm just saying that photos get leaked from movie sets all the time. Things that are taken out of context, per usual. I just don't want to seem like I'm flirting my tail off with you and have someone use that against you and further try to soil your reputation." My body softened.

"Are you flirting your tail off with me?" He looked back at Penny, whose lead rope was in his hands and shrugged. A smile formed on his lips.

"Maybe I am," he said, in his rugged, whiskey, leather deep voice.

"Maybe I don't care about anything else, or what they think, because I want this, too." I put the ball back in his court as I eagerly awaited his reply. I watched as he tucked Penny's rope back into the saddle horn.

"I don't want to be something that burns bright and disappears when filming wraps." I squinted at his words.

"What do you mean? Of course I do." How could he say I didn't know what I wanted?

"You've built a whole life outside of here. I don't expect you to trade that in because of a feeling. Because of a few weeks of stolen time in Dust Creek." I felt crushed by his words. Did the last few weeks mean nothing to him? Did I mean nothing to him?

"But Rhett, it's more than a feeling. I want to be here and continue to get to know you and—". He cut me off.

"You'd really stay? After the movie wraps? In Dust Creek?" There was a tone of disbelief in his voice, along with something else. Hurt. Fear. Denial. He was making sure that I didn't choose this life. That I didn't choose him. And I didn't understand it, but then, I felt God nudge my heart. Rhett was trying to push me away. He had things he had to figure out on his own. This wasn't the time nor the place. I wasn't going to argue my way into his life when he wasn't ready to accept me as I was.

"I mean, I think I'd like to, and—". He looked up at me and locked eyes.

"If this happens, Sadie, it will be for keeps. Not for a season." And with that, he turned and walked away. I felt stunned. I didn't know how to feel. I thought he just wanted to pump the brakes on our feelings, but as it was, the stove was turned down to a simmer. Other than a moment in the barn after we had just met, we'd not touched nor crossed any boundaries. I had only dreamt of his kiss. Was he pushing me away?

Tomorrow kicked off my final week of filming, and I only had one more scheduled session with him, which seemed like more of a formality at this point anyway. I felt nervous about it, seeing him again after our exchange. But something deep down told me that maybe he wasn't pushing me away. Maybe he was holding the line.

Closing the door of the cabin behind me, I needed to reflect on what had just happened. I reached for my phone, my finger hovering over the text message icon. But I didn't trust myself to text this one. I needed to call my friend. To pour my heart out and to, most importantly, gain insight on whatever that was that just had happened. Molly answered on the second ring.

"If this is about the cowboy, I'm already seated, both emotionally and physically." Her words brought a smile to my face.

"It's about the cowboy." My tone gave it away that I was upset.

"Oh no. What happened? Did you find out he likes to smash grapes with his feet and now he wants you to drink the foot-grape wine?"

"Worse," I said.

"What could be worse? Oh, my word. He's a collector of clown figurines? He showed you his 'trophy case' and all of their little painted faces followed you around the room? Run for the hills, girl. You do not need that in your life." No matter what could happen in my life, I knew Molly would always cheer me up.

"He gave me a speech," I said.

"Like, his practice speech for your nuptials?" Her words, however, were losing hope by the moment.

"Like a 'we need to put the brakes on,' speech. He said he wants to take things slow because we don't know each other. Then, he implied that surely I wouldn't want to stay in Dust Creek forever…" I felt the tears coming, and I didn't even know why. I chalked it up to PMS. Molly listened.

"Okay. So… That's actually really respectable. He doesn't want to be a fling. He wants more than that. But so do you." I thought for a moment.

"Well, of course I do. And I told him that, but he didn't seem on board."

"Tell me what happened after this. Word for word." I wiped my eyes.

"He said that if this happens, it will be for keeps." A loud thud was heard on the other end of the line. "Molly? Did you just fall?"

"I needed to lie down," she said. "Repeat that."

"Did you just—" She interrupted.

"No, repeat what Rhett said." I nodded.

"That if it happens, it will be for keeps."

"Did he say it slow?"

"Yes, sort of," I said.

"Eye contact?" I shrugged but agreed.

"Yes. He looked me dead in the eyes."

"Was there wind?" I laughed at her, knowing where this was going.

"Molly, why is this relevant?" I teased.

"I'm just trying to assess the severity of the situation," she stated.

"Well, here it is: He thinks when filming wraps soon, I'm going to leave and forget about this place and him." The words felt foreign coming out of my mouth.

"Would you do that? Leave and just... forget?" Molly asked.

"No, I wouldn't."

"Okay, then. Tell him that."

"But he put a halt to things already. Before they even began," I pleaded.

"No, he didn't. He put up a wall."

"It hurt my feelings," I admitted. "I don't want to have to fight my way into his life."

"You shouldn't have to," Molly agreed. "But Cowboy isn't asking you to fight. He said he just didn't want to do this halfway. He's measuring the depth of what you are looking for. Like they do in concrete for a house foundation."

"A house foundation? Where are you coming up with these analogies?" I teased. She let out a giggle.

"It must be because my boyfriend is a contractor."

"Your WHAT? Molly, you mean to tell me that you are dating someone and haven't shared with me every single little detail and how long has this been going on!?" I peppered her with questions until I had to take a breath.

"We met on the day of the awards show. I was planning on telling you but then the whole thing blew up, and..."

"You didn't want to upset me. You are such a good friend, Molly. But I want to hear about your joys, no matter what. Okay? Now spill!" The rest of the conversation was spent recalling facts about Molly's new boyfriend, Greg, who built track homes in Ohio. He was a tall five foot eight, and with Molly barely standing five foot two, she loved that she could wear any shoes she wanted. He liked to take her out on weekends to brunch, and then they strolled the city parks, hand in hand. It was a very sweet, pure relationship that was built on chemistry and communication. I couldn't help but realize Rhett and I only had that first part.

Before getting off the phone with Molly, I thanked her for her friendship. For getting me through these last few months. For being my ride or die in life.

"You're my golden girl," she said to me, before hanging up.

CHAPTER 22

Sadie

That night, I had dinner in my cabin. Turned out, all I had to do was request it in the privacy of my own room, and it arrived on my porch just a handful of moments later. Along with my food, which was all covered in those steel round things that fancy restaurants use to unveil your food, there was a small note on the tray.

> *There will be music tonight at the campfire.*
> *-Pat*

My heart skipped a beat. I knew Pat meant well. She liked me. I liked her, too. But at this very moment, I could see that she was very much interested in marrying off her son. While I also had an interest in that very matter, I hadn't decided if I felt up to listening to the music tonight—the music that filled up my mind and my heart and made me feel like I might burst from the overwhelming excitement that it made me feel towards this cowboy.

Rhett had a depth to his soul that I'd not seen in other men. Not that I'd gotten to know many on a personal level, but with Rhett, you saw it instantly. You felt it right away. He was deep. Tan. Tall. I shook the thoughts of his physical attractiveness from my head—there was so much more than that—and decided to pray.

"Lord, I know there is a difference between lust and love. Help me not cross that line, Lord. It's not his looks, though they certainly are a masterpiece of Your work. It's his heart, God. His soul. His mind. He's caring, he's kind, but most importantly, I feel like he's a protector. I think I'm falling in love with him, Lord. If this is not meant for me, if this is not meant for us, please let there be obstacles. Close every door that feels open. Lock the windows in case I try to slip through one of those, too. Lord, protect me from what's not mine. Despite my feelings that are growing by the day, I can and will walk away if You want me to. Having a glimpse of life with a respectable, godly man will have been worth the heartbreak and experience. In Your name, Amen."

My prayers went on for so long that by the time I was done, my food was cold. I picked at it, not having as much of an appetite as I thought. It was a tenderloin with mashed potatoes, green beans, and a gorgeous, colorful salad. I ate as much as I could, finding the food so flavorful that once I started tasting things, I couldn't put my fork down. On the edge of the tray, there was one more dish—a sliver of cheesecake with a handful of tiny, wild blueberries on top.

The sun started to wind down the day when I finished the food, setting the tray on the little cabin's kitchen counter. The chill that was initially in the air when I got here had left, replaced with warm nights. Tonight was especially so—there wasn't even a breeze in the air. It felt comfortable to wear a short sleeve shirt along with my jeans. I plucked the outfit I wore here, along with the sandals, out of my fresh laundry pile and put it on.

I still had the day's makeup on from the set. It wasn't a bad thing, but I preferred to be fresh faced normally, so it required some getting used to. However, it did make me look polished. Put together. The eyeliner and copious amounts of mascara made me look mysterious, so instead of removing it, I opted for a little mystery.

It wasn't until I was putting on a pair of good loop earrings that I realized I was actually going to the campfire to listen to his music, and I couldn't remember consciously deciding that. I stopped in my tracks. After a little reflection, I realized just how much I wanted to go. To see him. The nights here were almost done. I had this week of filming left, and in all the time I'd been here, I'd learned that Rhett strumming his guitar around the fire was not a common occurrence. I wanted to experience it again for a second time, even if it did make me pine for him like a tree in a forest.

When the sky finally turned dark, the only remaining light was a glow of the sun behind the vast mountains and the crackling, bright orange fire in the large ring. I looked around. Everyone who remained on set was in attendance. All of the ranch hands I'd seen around were there, sitting off to the sides, letting the guests take the chairs closest to the music. And, to my surprise, all of the chairs were taken, except one—right next to Rhett. *How convenient.*

Pat was walking around a tray that had marshmallow kits in small paper bags and a pile of roasting rods. Everyone was taking them. Some people even took more than one kit to make several s'mores. As I lingered, deciding just how much I wanted to hear the music tonight, if it was worth taking the seat next to Rhett, Pat came up to me with the tray, plucking off a kit and a roasting rod and handed them to me.

"Enjoy, Sadie," she said, with a knowing smile. Just then, Tonya heard my name and turned to me.

"Sadie? Are you joining us?" Her voice carried, silencing the chatter around us, while everyone who wasn't already looking in my direction was now.

"Yes," I whispered, "I just need to find a seat." I pretended I didn't see the seat next to Rhett, thinking that someone, *anyone* would be getting up or moving, but no one budged. Why would they? The music was just about to begin.

"I saved you a seat, Sadie." That whiskey voice rang smooth through my ears as all of the blood rushed to my face. I looked at Rhett, as he motioned beside him. He saved me a seat and just proclaimed it in front of everyone.

"Thank you," I said, as I felt eyes on me from everyone, but Rhett was the only one I cared about. Feeling Rhett's gaze was like having the sun shining directly on me. It made me feel warm. Happy. Energetic. Taking the seat beside him felt like a public display of affection. It felt like we were making it known to the world that we liked each other. It made the earlier conversation seem even more powerful. Molly was right—I read that whole script wrong. Rhett was falling just as hard for me as I was for him—he just was doing it in a way that protected his heart in the falling.

When I sat down, the first person I made eye contact with was Tonya. The look on her face went from confused to acceptance in rapid fire. I had seen Tonya unabashedly flirt with Rhett. He was gorgeous, and I wasn't surprised in the slightest. From what I understood, Tonya was single and looking to change that as soon as possible. I didn't blame her for shooting her shot with Rhett. But now, I felt like I'd betrayed Tonya in some way. I was washed with regret as I sat beside Rhett. Our chairs were only a few inches apart. They were all quite close to make room for more people in the fire ring. Tonya looked away from me.

I said a short, silent prayer under my breath. *Lord, I've been hurt, and I know how Tonya is feeling. Please help me make this right.* As I finished my prayer, Rhett strummed the first chord of a song and suddenly, all of my cares were washed away.

His song rang through the deepest valleys of my soul. It wasn't anything I'd heard before, and I considered it may have been an original that he had written himself. It was a tune about longing. Waiting for the return of a woman.

"There's a saddle sittin' empty, and a star filled sky, a wide open ridgeline, and a man askin' why..." His lyrics were so heartfelt and meaningful, tears formed in my eyes. Rhett had more talent with his music than anyone I'd ever heard on the radio, television, or in movies. He was so good at this that I felt stunned. When the song ended, I looked around at the bleary-eyed cast and crew. Everyone was affected by his song, myself included.

Rhett sat down his guitar and leaned back behind him, retrieving a blue banjo. I cocked an eyebrow at first, not knowing what was up his sleeve. But the second he started strumming, he sang a faster, folksy version of "It Is Well With My Soul" that I found myself tapping my foot to. Some people started clapping to the rhythm. I was hooked on his music, and there was a part of me that hoped I'd hear it for the rest of my life.

This couldn't end here, I thought to myself. This thing we had between us—it was more than attraction. It was more than a desire. My soul recognized his soul. Rhett was the man I wanted to be with. That I wanted to marry. But not right away or anything. I was still figuring things out. There was still so much I wanted to learn about him, and he about me. As he swapped out the banjo and again went back to his guitar, I considered the plans I had in my heart for the future and prayed that God would set my paths straight.

CHAPTER 23

Rhett

I wasn't thrilled with how the conversation ended with Sadie. There I went, creating chaos where there was none and making things a little too serious and heavy. It was what I did, and I'd been praying that I could lighten the mood tonight. Show Sadie that I might have made things a little intense earlier, but I could also be playful and fun. It started with saving her a seat.

Tonya was the first to ask me if it was available. I politely declined, saying I was saving it for Sadie. Tonya smiled awkwardly and in the dim light of the fire, I could see that I had caught her off guard. After a moment, she nodded her head.

"That's really cute," she offered. I shrugged.

"We will see if she accepts it," I said, with an undeniable anxiety in my voice.

"Is this something that's been going on?" she asked, starting to pry. I didn't know much about Tonya. I didn't know if she was asking earnestly because she had been the one flirting with me the last few weeks or if whatever I said would make it to the tabloids in the next hour. Sadie didn't deserve that. She needed privacy. Boundaries. After a moment, I shrugged it off.

"I don't really know," I said, which at that moment, felt entirely too true. Sadie and I had had something growing but up until recently, it had been physical attraction guiding the path. I didn't want to be ruled by the physical side of things, by the worldly desires of the flesh instead of the heavenly desires of my heart. Sure, Sadie and I had had a few near moments where our lips almost touched but at this point, I was thankful that it didn't happen. The Lord had much greater plans for this and call me old fashioned, but I wanted to wait for the perfect time to move when, or if, I did.

The air changed. I felt her before I saw her. When Sadie showed up at the fire pit, I suddenly lost my voice. She had hesitancy all over her face, rightfully so after our conversation earlier. I watched as my mom came in clutch, giving her the marshmallows and roasting rods. Now, she was locked in. But where would she decide to sit? All of the chairs were taken.

Except this one, of course. Finally, I spoke up. All of the eyes around us were settled on watching whatever this was unfolding. It was a bold move on my part, one that I probably should have thought through more, but after living my life so hesitantly out of fear of getting hurt, I wanted to give it a shot. Sadie accepted the seat, sitting down next to me. I couldn't help but notice she smelled like fresh lavender and vanilla. Her golden hair had a little curl to the bottom. She was wearing something that made her lips glossy and pink. As she leaned into the chair, her hand on the rest just inches from my hand on my armrest, it felt like the electricity between us could power a *Piggly Wiggly*. The biggest accomplishment was my restraint from putting my hand on hers.

I couldn't take it any longer. If I didn't busy my hands and mind with strumming the guitar, I would have surely started rambling to her about something I might have regretted later. I just wasn't used to feeling so unhinged around a person. I needed to stay in control of these urges to flirt and hold her hand in this public setting. To let God keep my mind, my heart, and my actions in check. I was starting to surprise myself with these feelings as they grew by the moment.

After I sang a couple songs, switching it up to the banjo for one, I went back to my guitar and sang something new. Something I had just been inspired to write in the last week. It was a song about Sadie, about her impending departure, and how I already felt about it. The only eyes I saw while I was playing it were my mom's and dad's. I knew that they knew how I was feeling. This song was going to surprise them, as I never sang things like this to guests. I always kept it light. I kept it spiritual. Kept it refreshing. This song was a little more sad. It was a little more of my own self looking in a mirror at a reflection I didn't recognize. I was a man falling in love for the first time and preparing myself for heartbreak as it came to a close before it even started.

CHAPTER 24

Sadie

As the music came to a close, I watched all of Rhett's movements out of the corner of my eye, as he collected his guitar and banjo. He was readying himself to leave. Tomorrow was the start of the last full filming day. I still had one session with Rhett this week, despite my scenes with the horses almost being done filming. It felt like more of a formality, though I was thankful for it. I was blessed to have the time with him on my schedule. Any time I could steal away with him was enjoyable.

Rhett lingered, holding the necks of his instruments while looking forward at the flames. Everyone around us was starting to shuffle out. Tonya was the first to go; she gave me a smile and nod before she did. I smiled back. I felt relief from the brief interaction.

"I guess I better turn in," I said, breaking the silence between us. Letting him know that the time at the fire ring was running out. That tomorrow would be one step closer to the movie being wrapped.

"Sadie," he said, which sounded more like a prayer than a plea. "What I said earlier, I..." I paused my breathing while my heart beat faster. "I'm sorry for saying you wouldn't stay. But we both know you have your whole life in front of you and... That would be crazy, right?" Immediately, I felt the tone sour once again. I peeled my eyes off of Rhett and looked at the dancing, flickering flames of the firelight. While I watched the flames, it came to my mind what was happening. Everything was adding up. Rhett was pushing me away.

"Do you want me to leave?" I asked him point blank. His face suddenly looked anguished. After a time of silence, I looked away again, while he worked whatever it was out in his head.

"I don't want you to leave, Sadie. Of course, I don't. Heck, I don't even understand how this has happened, but I'm falling in love with you, Sadie." His words were like the sparkling clangs of a windchime on a wraparound porch on a summer evening. Comforting, nourishing to my soul, but gone with the breeze.

"Then why do you push me away, Rhett? I feel the same way. I'd like to try this with my whole heart." As I put my words on the line, Rhett's eyes wandered back to me. In this light, they looked like the color of honey. The color of the saddle that Penny wore. The color of warm, worn leather.

"I can't ask you to give up whatever is next, for me." I shook my head, not having anything on the calendar yet, and I didn't know if I ever would again. That's how Hollywood worked. One day you' were in; the next... you were out. I was blessed by this role, but I had no idea what, if anything, would come from it.

"I wouldn't be giving anything up, Rhett. I think you have a different idea of me than I do, and to be honest, I don't like feeling like I have to plead with you here."

"I'm sorry, Sadie." He took a deep breath and put his head in his hands for a moment, then removed his cowboy hat and revealed his gorgeous head of hair. "I've been praying about this and... My hangup is putting up guardrails every time I think hurt is on the horizon."

"You've done this before?" Rhett shrugged and nodded.

"I've never dated. Never felt strongly enough about anyone to try. I've never... fallen in love before." The words lingered between us. If that meant what I thought it meant... I was his first love. The weight of that was enormous because I was feeling the same way. Even with the stain of Tommy on my past, I had never felt like this before. I had never loved before.

"I've never fallen in love either." My words trailed off before he turned and looked at me suddenly. "Before this." And at that, Rhett let out a deep sigh. Laughter and a smile took over his face.

"Lord, help us," Rhett said, praying to God above.

The night ended for most of the crew and cast, with almost everyone going off to their trailers and cabins for the night. Billy and Pat lingered in chairs in the back. Though they had their backs to us as they watched for shooting stars, there was a comfort knowing they were present.

"Tell me something about you," I prompted Rhett, who added another log to the fire from the pile next to his chair.

"Oh, that's a hard question to answer on the spot. What do you want to know?"

"I want to know why you just answered a question with a question," I said, poking him in the arm. Doing so almost jammed my finger, with his muscles being so firm. *Why are they so firm?*

"My favorite color is blue, like your eyes," he said, glancing over at me. I was grinning like an idiot already. "My favorite food is Italian everything. And, I like to think of myself as a pretty good cook."

"Really? Isn't that convenient, I happen to *love* to be cooked for. What is your best dish?"

He ran his fingers through his thick, lustrous, dark brown hair that was flattened from his cowboy hat. The top of his forehead was lighter than the rest of his face, being shielded from the sun. I smiled while he named off a few dishes, none of the items I'd ever heard of before. "So, mostly Italian things."

"Extra cheese, and I'm there."

"Are you inviting yourself over to my kitchen for a meal, *Hollywood?*" I blushed and nodded.

"Maybe I am, *Wranglers.*" I laughed at the sound of his nickname coming out of my lips and snorted. The snort surprised me, but Rhett started busting up harder than I thought possible for a serious guy like him. Even Pat and Billy could be heard snickering from where they were.

"You are cute when you're embarrassed, you know that?" he asked.

"I don't know how you'd know that, because I've never been embarrassed around you."

"Sure, you have," he quipped.

"Oh really? Like when? Name one time. I'll wait."

"Like the first time we met. I don't know about what, but your cheeks were the color of a strawberry lemonade."

"You've really got a lot of nerve comparing me to juice," I teased. "I'm more of a dessert. Maybe even a fine wine." He shrugged.

"You're fancy, that's for sure. But I don't drink, so it wasn't the first thing to come to mind." It was refreshing knowing that he abstained from alcohol, considering my past with Tommy.

"I don't drink, either. It gives me a headache," I offered. He nodded.

"I had a bit of a phase where I enjoyed whiskey every evening. It started innocently enough with guests asking me to have a drink with them, but then I'd have another and before I knew it, I was sleeping in late and staying up later. I don't like the party lifestyle—not for me, anyways. I ain't gonna judge what anyone else enjoys."

"You really are the whole package, you know that?" I asked. He turned to me, his face just mere inches from mine as he leaned my direction.

"Oh yeah?"

"Yeah." He leaned in and kissed me on the cheek, slowly pulling away.

"It's past my bedtime, Hollywood. I better get up so I can feed the horses before you and Penny start makin' movies with 'em." I internally groaned. I was enjoying this time with him way too much, but he was right; it was getting very late.

"I better get to bed, too. This was nice. Thank you, Rhett." And just like that, the night was over. But not before he leaned in slowly, and his lips landed on my forehead. He left without another word.

That night, back in my cabin, I checked my messages. I had a whole slew of them from Janie asking me to call her. I checked the time—it was an hour earlier in California, and I knew she was a night owl, so I dialed her number.

"Sadie," she answered on the second ring.

"Hey, Janie. I'm sorry I didn't call you earlier. I just got your messages."

"No problem. I figured you've been out tonight. Just a few more days on set, right?" There was something behind her voice. Something I hadn't heard in a long time: excitement.

"Yes, I have about a week left, give or take." Janie cracked open a can, and I would've bet my paycheck it was Diet Coke. She could have never been seen without one in her hand.

"Give or take? Are things getting held up?" Her voice switched to concern.

"Well, no. Things are moving right along, actually. I was just thinking I'd stick around for a few days after we wrapped up and see more of Wyoming." *Aka see more of Rhett.*

"Uh huh. Well, I've got a better idea," she teased, the excitement in her voice boiling over. "A movie still was posted by the production company of you all dolled up in your head-to-toe cowgirl look. You'll never guess who has just contacted us and asked if you will come do a guest role on their show?" I actually did have a guess, but it didn't make me any less confused.

"What does he want from me?" I felt myself stomping my foot in shock.

"Who?" Janie sounded confused.

"Tommy!" I shouted, immediately covering my mouth and saying a short prayer to help control my anger.

"Well, it wasn't Tommy that asked. It was the creator of the show, Bob Black." That was still too close for comfort.

"Is Bob Black living under a rock? Does he not know that Tommy is out to destroy my career and soil my reputation?"

"Does this mean you're not interested?" Janie asked honestly.

"I'm a little surprised you would suggest I take such an offer, right into the lion's den like that." I set the phone down, putting her on speaker and crossing my arms while I wore a path in the floor from pacing.

"I never said you should take it. In fact, I would advise that you don't take it," she said, slyly.

"What do you mean? Isn't this why you asked me to call? You were so excited." My confusion was through the roof.

"Sadie, that was only part one of why I wanted you to call me. And really, that helps me reinforce some boundaries. I will let that studio know we are not interested."

"Thank you, Janie. So, what else? I don't mean to speed things up, but it is getting late here and..." I trailed off.

"I know, I'm sorry. Okay, here's the main reason. The real reason, let's say."

"I'm waiting?" I said with a laugh. This build up was insane.

"*Gummy,* the shark movie, wants you back!" My jaw nearly fell to the floor as tears welled in my eyes. Not only was that set to be a huge summer blockbuster, but the paycheck alone would secure my future if I never got another role again.

"Yes, tell them yes!" I shouted, jumping up and down. Then, the questions started rolling off my tongue. "What changed?" Janie sipped her soda.

"Honestly, I think that movie still. The fact that you are working on another project. I think they felt like you were untouchable after the whole big... You know. Now, the cooties have worn off, so to speak."

"If anyone has cooties, it should be Tommy. Is he still on his social media tour of tarnishing me?" Janie let out a sigh.

"Yes, I'm afraid he is. But, people have started to defend you in the comments. People are turning their back on him. This will pass, Sadie. You working on this movie is the best thing for your career." As she spoke, my mind started to race, thinking about the shark schedule.

"Wait. Did *Gummy* change its filming dates? Because if not, it would start in just a few days..." This had to be different. I wanted to stay here for a while. I wanted to stay with Rhett. Now, I was going ahead with his prophecy about my leaving the second filming had wrapped. The thought put a pit in my gut.

"No, that's the last reason why I called. I've been texting with Tonya, and they think they can have you wrapped up in three days and have you back on a plane the night of the third. You need to report to Melbourne two days after that. That gives you one day to freshen up in the hotel, read the script, and so on. Just wait until you see the lodging setup! You're never going to want to leave, Sadie." Three days. Just three days of back-to-back filming, and I'd be leaving here. Leaving Wyoming. Leaving Rhett and a piece of my heart with him.

I thanked Janie for the call, while she hung up to make the contractual arrangements, telling me that she'd have something for me to sign in the morning. She would find someone to give it to me, and I would deliver it to them in Australia in just a few days' time. My mind wandered to Rhett. When would I see him? When would I tell him? After climbing into bed, I thanked God for the day. For my many countless blessings. For the opportunity of a lifetime to shoot this movie, and now my dreams were coming true with *Gummy.* But I couldn't help but wonder if it was still my dream, after all this time. After all of this rejection. After enduring so many trials by this very industry that was now trying to take me back into the fold that I willingly just agreed to jump right back into. Doing so would mean leaving here even earlier than I had wanted to. *Lord, will I leave here and never return?* My heart was as heavy as an anchor, as I prayed myself to sleep.

CHAPTER 25

Sadie

Rhett was nowhere to be found the next day. Pat brought me a manilla envelope to my cabin, that was just stamped "Contract" in bold red letters. It must have weighed five pounds. My heart sank, wondering if she had opened it. Did she print it? I wondered. Then, on the back of the envelope, I found a sticker for the company that sent it. Whew. It was overnighted. Impressive, to get it all the way out here. But still. The implications of this envelope, and now that Pat knew I was committing to something else—I wondered what was going on in her mind.

CHAPTER 26

Sadie

Day two was finally over, my heart longing to see Rhett but once again, he didn't materialize. I was starting to wonder if I needed to go knock on his cabin door, but I didn't know which one was his. There was a cabin way out further up the river. It had a light on inside. I could see it from my cabin's porch at night. As I looked at it, my breathing slowed to a snail's pace. My mind was soothed by the sounds of the river. A small breeze was floating through the air, pulling my hair back slightly. I closed my eyes and felt the world under my feet. I felt the heaviness of the day wash away. *Lord, I'm head over heels for this man. Please, let me have the chance to say goodbye to him.*

CHAPTER 27

Rhett

It might have been the dumbest thing to ever happen in the history of the world. Especially for a guy like me, who had been walking in boots on uneven ground my entire life. After I kissed Sadie on the forehead, I was walking back to my cabin at the end of the river. I felt like I was floating on clouds. Thanking the Lord for every step I took, when BAM! The heel of my boot slipped on a river rock that was in my path, and my ankle moved *just right,* twisting it into oblivion. I was able to get into my cabin and remove my boots before it started swelling up. The pain was awful for such a minor contortion. I couldn't believe my luck, especially with Sadie only having a few days left.

I called my dad, and he said he would fill in for me for a few days with the horses. I iced it as much as I could. I could barely walk on it. Could barely put any weight on it at all for two days straight. On the morning of the third day, it felt better. Manageable. I didn't like taking meds—I felt like they just added poisons to my body—but I took some anti-inflammatory pain relievers and felt like I could handle the work load.

The second I started walking outside, I felt like I'd made a mistake. It still hurt, bad, but "mind over matter," I kept telling myself. I had to get this behind me. I wanted to see Sadie.

As I reached the horse corral, the movie set was already ramping up for the day. Sadie was standing at the saloon, holding a Yellowboy replica gun. Her eyes widened as she saw me, but I couldn't read what her expression was. There was a woman touching up her makeup. *I didn't know 1800's women wore so much eyeliner,* I laughed to myself. Sadie looked gorgeous with the makeup, but she was the most beautiful woman in the world without it.

I leaned against the corral after my chores were complete, taking the weight off of my right ankle. I heard the director yell, "CUT!" and a set of old-style western lace up boots started running towards me. I smiled to myself, turning around, but my heart sank as I was met with Sadie, who's eyes were filled with tears.

"Where have you been, Rhett?" she whispered, pulling me away from the corral. I winced in pain. "Oh, my goodness. Are you hurt?" I nodded.

"The other night, after the... campfire, I twisted my ankle pretty bad. I'm honestly embarrassed at how injured I am right now. Could barely walk the last two days." Sadie's eyes went from upset to concern.

"Rhett, there is something I need to tell you." The tone in her voice sounded desperate.

"Okay, what is it? Are you okay?"

"I'm okay. But something came up. Another movie—one I was actually set to do before. They want me back now, and... I'm leaving tonight." Tears were streaming from her eyes now. My heart dropped to my gut. I thought we'd have more time.

"Tonight? Are you sure?" I knew that there was a late-night flight to Denver, as the pilots never wanted to overnight in Dust Creek, but I was still in disbelief. This wasn't how it was supposed to go.

"I know. I don't want to go like this, so soon. But I need this job and taking it means I can support myself and..." And she was worried about me. Because I had said bonehead things to her about her leaving and not coming back and... *I'm a jerk.*

"Of course you do, Sadie. You deserve every opportunity to come your way." I wiped the tears from her cheeks, searching my heart for what to say. Praying for wisdom on how to behave.

"Thank you, Rhett." She stifled her tears. "I'm just upset I didn't get to meet the raccoons yet." She gave me a soft smile before turning somber again. "I want that movie..." She trailed off, locking eyes on me again. "But I want this, too. Can there be both?" I took her hands in mine, as someone from the set started telling her it was time to start again.

"Can I drive you to the airport tonight?" I asked as her eyes lit up.

"Yes. I would love that. We are shooting the rest of my scenes today, so I have to go. But will you wait for me here tonight?"

"I will wait for you forever." The words escaped my lips so fast, but here was the thing: For once in my life, I was ready to lead with my heart. I wasn't going to be afraid of getting hurt anymore. My mom was right—hurt was the price of loving. I had fallen hard for Sadie, and the experience alone was beautiful and worth the pain of whatever came next.

CHAPTER 28

Sadie

"You take your kind, and you get back to where you came from." I looked dead in the eye at Scott, who was playing Jacob Marks, an old west outlaw. "Because I guess you ain't heard—I'm the Belle of Bitter Creek, and I ain't goin' to stand here and beg you for the honor. The only one that I care about how I look in front of is the Lord, and by golly, I'm going to be white as snow in His sight when we meet at the pearly gates. Now you best get on and get on quick, because I got the law comin' after you." Scott spit to my left, looked me up and down, and sauntered off.

"Cut!" And just like that, it was over. Tonya was immediately at my side to congratulate me.

"Another perfect scene! It's almost like you've done this before," she teased, giving me a side hug as we both rushed to the hair, makeup, and wardrobe trailer.

"Thank you for everything, Tonya," I said, as we tore through the door, and I unlaced my boots and unbuttoned the elaborate riding skirt, quickly running behind a screen and changing into my jeans and t-shirt. My dolled-up hair and makeup would just have to go with me to Melbourne.

"I hope we work together again, Sadie. I know you're moving on to bigger and better things, but I mean that. This movie is really going to be something. I can feel it in my bones." Her words electrified me as I reflected on the movie we had just made.

"I can feel it too, Tonya." I leaned in for a hug. "Stay in touch, please." She had my number.

"And will you be, um, staying in touch with anyone else?" She winked.

"I'm praying so." Giving her a smile, I took the steps out of the trailer and practically ran to my cabin. Inside, everything had already been packed for me, not that there was much to begin with. Sitting on top of my suitcase was the pair of cowgirl boots that Pat lent me when I got here. When I turned to wheel my suitcase out of the cabin, Pat appeared.

"Darling, I know you're running out of here, but I just wanted to say goodbye." She leaned in for a hug, and I hugged her back as hard as I could.

"You are just my favorite," I said, pulling back, and slipping on a zip up sweatshirt.

"Don't forget the shoes. They look better on you than they will ever look on me. Besides, I hear there are snakes in the outback. You might need some strong leather to protect your ankles." Tears welled up in my eyes. I really wasn't ready to leave.

"Speaking of ankles," I laughed, as Rhett appeared in the doorway. He hobbled in and retrieved the handle of my suitcase and the boots. Pat squeezed my arm and left without another word.

"Ready?" Rhett asked, his eyes looking as lost as mine.

"No, I'm not," I laughed again, but more emotion was behind my voice.

We walked to his truck, which was just a little ways over, and he opened the door for me. I climbed in, inspecting my surroundings. It was suspiciously clean from the last time I rode in it when Billy picked me up from the airport, and it smelled like the leather was just freshly conditioned. The windows were sparkling, clear of bugs and debris.

"Did you spend the day cleaning?" I asked with a smile across my face as he climbed in the driver's side. I never thought I'd see him turn red but finally, here he was, mildly blushing.

"Nah, it's always like this. What? You think just because I'm covered in dirt head to toe at any given minute, my truck isn't spotless?" As he spoke, I noticed just how clean he looked, too. And he was wearing a different hat. Dirt free. His shirt was crisply tucked into his jeans with a different belt. It looked fancy, with a large silver buckle.

I took in every part of him that I could, my eyes trying to imprint this to my memory. There was so much I wanted to say. To say I wanted to keep in touch was an understatement. But before I knew it, the long, quiet drive up and down dirt roads was over. We were in town, the flashing light of the airport beacon in my view, as we slowed to a stoplight.

"Rhett, I—". I turned to him, and my face was met with his lips on mine. Right there, at a stoplight, in a one stoplight town, on a two-lane road, smack dab in the middle of Rosa's Dairy and Tom's Butcher Shop, Rhett kissed me. I didn't know how long I sat there, feeling the most handsome man's lips, but it might have lasted forever if a truck hadn't honked behind us, letting us know the light was green.

Rhett pulled away, hesitantly, and hit the gas pedal to go forward. I was stunned by his beautiful mouth on mine. The excitement of the moment would surely get me through the next three months on scene in Australia.

As we slid into the airport, he pulled right up to the curb and quickly jumped out and unloaded my suitcase. We still hadn't spoken since he kissed me. Before I knew it, he was opening my door again. I stepped off of the running boards and into his arms where we hugged for as long as I could. It sounded like the plane engine was turning on, and I knew we only had seconds to spare.

"Don't worry. They wait for you out here. Heck, they are probably so excited to fly you tonight that the pilots won't even budge till you step on." I smiled at his words, not wanting to even think about the plane right now. Not even wanting this to be real. I looked up at him, thinking he might kiss me again, but instead, we locked eyes which felt even more intimate.

"I'll be back, Rhett. After—" He cut me off.

"You don't need to make me any promises, Sadie. Just knowing you has meant the world to me." He kissed me on the forehead and stepped back from our embrace.

"But I want to, Rhett," I said, pleading at him with my eyes. He took another step back. "Take a step towards me, Rhett. I want to do this whole thing. I mean it." Rhett just stepped back again and smiled.

"You have the whole world in front of you, Hollywood. And you deserve so much more than what I can give you. Here I am, living in the middle of nowhere Wyoming. You belong under the glittering lights, and all I have is the twinkling stars." Tears welled in my eyes.

"I want the stars. I want you, Rhett."

"I can promise you this, Sadie: I will be here for the rest of my life. That's all there is to it. But I want you to go out and dream big. I want to see your name in lights. I want you to be the biggest star Hollywood has ever known. Follow your dreams, Sadie. Don't worry about me." I was on the verge of ugly crying because I loved Rhett, too, and at this moment, I felt at peace with his words. Maybe the timing wasn't right? I wasn't sure. But what I did know was his encouragement of my dreams meant everything.

"But what about your dreams, Rhett? Will you be chasing them?" He looked down for a moment and looked back up.

"I already have. I met the woman of my dreams, and I fell in love. Then tonight, I kissed her. Consider this mission complete."

A woman wearing a silk scarf around her neck stepped outside of the airport.

"Ms. Clark? The plane is waiting for you." She returned inside.

"Wow, you really meant what you said. It's almost like I'm flying private." I let out a laugh and wiped my tears.

"When the town is this small, and everyone is in everyone's business, nothing can be private." Rhett smiled and I started rolling inside, looking back one more time.

"I love you too, you know," I said with a half-smile, more tears welling. He nodded.

"Go, be the woman that God created you to be. You're going to do big things, Sadie." I wheeled my bag inside, tears flowing down my cheeks as I walked through security. The agent asked if I had anything in my pockets. I reached in my pockets.

Before I could shake my head, I felt something in a wrapper. Pulling it out, it was a strawberry candy.

Someone tagged my bag and gave me a stub for picking it up at my final destination. Someone else said they loved me in that movie last summer. A woman asked if I was okay. Out of the fog or bright, sterile lighting and smells of jet fuel as I walked onto the tarmac, I nodded yes. I was okay. I would be okay. I wasn't sure what God had in store for me, but He had folded the corner of this page for now. Maybe I'd come back to it, as I yearned to do. Maybe Rhett wouldn't want to, for whatever reason. But God was writing the script, and I had faith that in the end, it would be better than I could have ever imagined.

CHAPTER 29

Sadie

In Australia, I was welcomed by a red carpet. Literally, someone met me at the airport and had me walk over a thick, plush, red rug. It was silly, and frankly, a little embarrassing after I had just spent several weeks in Wyoming living in a different world. Yes, I'd been credited to a few roles. No, I was not a deity, and did not want to be treated as such by random people. If only that was the only thing that was off.

A casting assistant introduced himself as Eddie. "I'm going to be getting you to the movie site," he said eagerly. "

Once they escorted me to the car, which was a stretch Hummer, complete with a mini fridge, bar, and *Hors d'oeuvres,* I got comfortable in my seat, thinking how much I could go for a glass of Pat's lavender lemonade right now. The city noises and traffic made me yearn for the sound of the roaring river.

There was another woman in the Hummer, and she introduced herself as my makeup artist. She and I would be working closely together for the next few months. She just couldn't wait to dive in, and she proceeded to get up from her seat and sit next to me, with her giant kit of makeup in tow.

As I sat there, she removed all of the movie makeup I'd been wearing for the last twenty-four hours. That felt great. I felt like I could finally breathe, in fact. I thanked her, touching the softness of my skin after she used the remover wipes. When she then took out a kit to color match me, I declined.

"I'll just go fresh faced today," I said, waving off her makeup brushes and wands. She responded with a laugh.

"Oh, no you won't." Her thick accent made her sound more playful than she looked. I gave her a confused expression. "You are the star of the movie. We can't let you be seen like this by the cast and crew. That will set a dangerous precedent. As it is, you were a tricky choice."

"Tricky?" I figured I knew what she was referring to— all of my drama with Tommy—but I didn't understand why the makeup artist was bringing it up. Her sentiments were echoed by Eddie, who was nodding his head.

"You were...complicated," he said, smiling as if that would alleviate the weirdness of this conversation. "You are the most beautiful woman in Hollywood, but with the mark on your reputation with Tommy, it was really hard for the movie executives to circle back to you." The shock rose to my face. I already had known these things, but now, hearing them spoken plainly to me, I couldn't for the life of me figure out how I got this so wrong. "By the way, we still haven't received that contract back from you." The contract that Janie had told me to give in person when they picked me up. The contract that I had stuffed in my small suitcase, which was sitting just inches from me on the nearest seat. The contract that, once I handed it over, meant this deal would be as good as permanent.

"Oh, I haven't?" I asked, trying to buy myself some time to figure out just what kind of rogue move I was pulling. After all, I'd just flown across the world to get here. I'd just left everything behind that felt right, to be surrounded by a couple of people who were treating me like a pawn, instead of a person.

"No, you haven't. And I'm afraid I'm going to need it before we get there. You see, this is highly unusual that we fly you out here before we receive it and—" I cut him off with a burst of laughter. They looked at me like I'd gone mad. Maybe I'd finally lost it. After all these months of being tormented by this industry and then being treated like gold on the indie side of things, it was no coincidence that I was here. God needed to show me the things I prayed for to realize why I didn't want them.

"I guess you'll have to turn this thing around and take me back to the airport, then." I couldn't imagine the turning radius on a stretch Hummer would be good, and, it turned out I was right about that.

"Excuse me? To turn around, we would have to drive another thirty kilometers before an opportunity arose." I just shrugged in reply.

"Turn around. There is no contract. There is no deal." I pulled the strength from my inner being as I spoke plainly to them. The makeup artist looked like her jaw might dislocate from her face. Eddie's face turned red as he started furiously texting. The driver was signaled to turn around at the nearest opportunity. It was a long ride back to the airport, where I was left on the curb, with my luggage and dignity intact.

I knew what I needed to do. I knew where I wanted to be. I pulled out my phone, which I only just now realized was at 1%. I hadn't charged it since I left Wyoming. It was going to die at any minute. Likely, I could have only made one phone call before it went dead.

"Hi, Molly."

"Sadie? Um, hi! How are you? Is everything okay?" I heard a hammer pounding in the background.

"I'm in Australia," I said, in my own disbelief that I thought this was ever a good idea.

"Australia? What about Wyoming?"

"It's sort of a long story, but... I just walked away from *Gummy.*"As I said the words, I realized my voice wasn't shaking. My hands were still. This wasn't a regret. I felt empowered. My phone warned me that it was about to go dead as I walked back inside of the airport.

"Hold on—let me step outside. I'm visiting my *boyfriend*at work." The happiness in her voice was a joy to hear.

"Molly, my phone is about to die. I'll find a charger and call you back."

"Okay, but stay on the line until it does. I want to hear this." So, I told her what happened. Miraculously, my phone hadn't gone dark yet. "You know what I'm going to ask, Sadie." Molly was so much more than my best friend—she was also a therapist to me, constantly pushing me out of my comfort zone.

"Maybe, but you should ask anyway, just to be sure." She giggled.

"What happens next?" And the phone went dead. I took a deep breath, looking at its black screen. Up above me stood the flight board. I scanned for the next flight going back to the USA. I looked behind me at the doors that led to a new country I'd never been to, and then my eyes went back to the flights. I prayed that God would guide me in this moment.

CHAPTER 30

Rhett

If you love something, let it go. I think that's how the phrase goes. I saw it once on a bumper sticker. The car had out-of-state plates. Two unusual sights for Dust Creek—most of the cars around here are so rusted up, there ain't much left for a bumper sticker to hold onto. That, and other than here at the Broken Arrow, we ain't much of a destination like other towns.

Take Iron Spur, Wyoming—they have a nightly rodeo, most days of the year. That's a draw. Or Maple Haven, Wyoming. I've heard the fall colors alone are worth the trip. Maybe I'll go there someday. Maybe I'd like to see more of the world. Maybe I'd even come back with a better understanding of why I am the way that I am.

All of these crazy thoughts have been racing through my head since I dropped Sadie off at the airport all those nights ago. If I had to guess, she'd been gone for eleven days, sixteen hours, and forty-five minutes. I checked my watch. Forty-seven minutes.

The day she told me she was leaving, with tears in her eyes, I knew then that Sadie was the one. I couldn't explain it— it was like a feeling of adrenaline, peace, and sadness for her leaving, all at once. After all of these years, I'd finally found the one. The woman I would love for the rest of my life. Except the chances of us being together were so slim, I had to accept that it most likely would not happen. But we still had that ride to the airport together. We still had our goodbye. There was no more time for living in fear—this was only a time to act.

I didn't plan on kissing her—at least not at first. But as the car ride went on, I couldn't think of a reason why I shouldn't. She had wanted to kiss me in the crumbling barn. I had wanted to kiss her so many times before that.

The kiss was, in a word, magnetic. We were lost in time while our lips touched—lost in love. It was pure. It was everything in that moment.

Now, as I contemplated my life going forward, I knew that Sadie was living her best life. Movie stills had already dropped from Australia. Her hair was styled in waves. She was wearing a long sleeve wet suit with shorts. Her skin looked sun kissed. She wasn't smiling in any of the photos.

When Sadie said she wouldn't leave after filming, that was before she had the opportunity of a lifetime. I didn't want her to turn that down for me. I couldn't allow her to do that. But as I reflected now, I found myself wondering what would have become of things if she had turned it down, on her own free will.

"Rhett?" My dad, Billy, tapped me on my shoulder. I was brought back to the present moment, where I was holding the lead rope for Blackjack, a black and white horse with a cream-colored mane and tail.

"Hey," I said, pretending to not be as caught off-guard as I was.

"There is someone here to see you." He pointed off in the distance to a black SUV driving up the dirt road, towards the ranch. My heart stopped. Who could it be? As the vehicle got closer, I saw the face of a crew member I recognized. I let out a breath. Did I think it was going to be Sadie coming back for me or something? I shook my head as if doing so would shake these insane thoughts loose.

The SUV came to a stop slowly. "They are here to see me? Why?" I asked my dad in confusion. What could the crew ever want with me?

"That's what they said when they called a few minutes ago. Beats me." He shrugged but stayed put. His steady presence lingered.

"Rhett?" the man called out. I remembered his face from the movie crew, but I couldn't put a name to him. "Matt Miller. I don't believe we have formally met." He reached out and shook my hand. "I'm the music supervisor for the movie, and something has been nagging at me this whole time, but I didn't have the guts to ask you in person when we were all here working every day."

"Alright, Matt. Go ahead, shoot." Matt smiled.

"You see, there is a song that I'd love to put to a specific scene, where our Belle is saying her final lines." I noticed he called Sadie by her character name and not her real name, which I found myself overthinking. I wanted to hear her name. I wanted her to be brought up.

"And which song is that?" I asked, having a feeling it was one of mine, or else he wouldn't have driven all the heck out here to chat with me about it.

"That song you sang not too long ago, around the campfire ring. I can't quite remember the lyrics, but I remember how it made me feel." I nodded.

"There's a saddle sittin' empty..." I said the words aloud and Matt nodded his head.

"That's the one. What do you say? Could we record it for the movie?"

"I suppose so. Let me just get the lyrics written up and some music notes jotted down for the man that will be singing it." I turned. Matt objected.

"No, no. Rhett, we want *you* to sing it. Of course, there would be some legal jargon involved with this agreement, and you'd get compensated, of course. But ideally, you would be performing it for the movie." Now I was really blown off my seat. I never set out to be some fancy music star. I didn't do things like that. I had no need for fame and glory. But somewhere in my heart, God was nudging me to accept this opportunity. He gave me the gift of song, and now I could honor Him in this Christian movie with it.

"I'll do it," I said, shaking his hand. My dad let out a breath and laughed.

"My boy, I couldn't be prouder of you."

*****

The next day, Matt returned with a contract and three people who needed a cabin space to set up a recording studio. Since some of the cast and crew were still filing out, my mom offered them the only cabin that was ready: Sadie's. As I led them to the space that housed the woman I fell in love with, I watched them set up acoustics. Special wall coverings. More equipment than I'd ever seen in my life.

When they were finished, there was a stool for me to sit on with my guitar and a microphone in front of it. They requested a few test strums of the sound so they could tweak their systems. This went on for quite some time. I thought I'd sit there forever when finally, Matt gave me a thumbs up and said to start singing.

CHAPTER 31

Sadie

As I strolled out of the airport, I closed my eyes, feeling the ground beneath my feet. Taking in the sound of the wind around me. The feeling of being back here.

I waved when I saw my ride, the woman's wide smile beaming back at me as I nearly cried in relief.

"Sadie," Pat said, taking me in for a hug. "I'm so glad you are back here with us." I nodded in reply.

"You have no idea how good it feels to be back." I took a deep breath, relaxing myself, as we climbed into the truck, my suitcase in the back truck bed.

The last few days had been a whirlwind. Something I was starting to get used to. From Australia, I booked a mishmash of flights to get me back to Ohio where I spent a handful of days praying about my decisions. Janie, my manager, was on board with everything and put out feelers that I was interested in only working indie movies for the Christian production companies. Within a day, I got several bites. One company said they were building a role for me. Another offered me a project that they were about to start casting for. And the production company that I had just worked for on *The Belle of Bitter Creek* offered me a three-movie contract in a western series, filmed in Wyoming, not far from Dust Creek. I accepted that without another thought.

Before making any other plans, I spent some time with my parents and Molly. Her new boyfriend was an absolute gem of a guy, and I could tell immediately that things were moving quite quickly. Seeing her was refreshing to my soul and grounding in my mind. Being back home always brought me peace.

On my last day home, I made the announcement that I was moving to Wyoming. I had already called a real estate agent when I got back to Ohio, and I was going to sell my condo in California and buy a humble piece of land in Dust Creek. In fact, I had already found the land, and I excitedly recounted the details to my loved ones. It had a small cabin on it, a horse pasture, and a seasonal creek. There was a working water well, established trees, and a neighbor who raised feral raccoons.

"Excuse me," Molly objected, as everyone including her new boyfriend sat around me in my parents' living room. "Did you say *feral + raccoons* in the same sentence, as in, this is a good thing?" I laughed so hard I snorted.

"If you raise them from cubs, it's really no big deal." I shrugged.

"If they go out of town, will you be stepping in to feed them? Or, if they run out of garbage for the *cubs* to eat, do they borrow a few cups from yours?" Molly had a love of using air quotes and always had the best questions. At the end of the night, when we'd all had a great laugh, I said goodnight to Molly and her boyfriend, hugging her tightly.

"I expect a visit once I'm settled in," I whispered in her ear. She gave me one more squeeze before leaving.

"I'll be waiting for some paint swatches to approve for the guest bedroom."

After they left, I retreated to the back porch to make a phone call. I found the only number online that was listed for the Broken Arrow and dialed without another thought. Afterwards, I thanked the Lord for all of it. There wasn't a single situation in the last few months of my life that could have been skipped for this outcome. While I praised Him, the crickets were chirping, a warm breeze was in the air, and the sound of my mother's windchimes were lulling me into comfort, as I softly rocked back and forth in the swinging egg chair.

Now, as I rode in the truck with the welcome sound of Pat's laughter and excitement, we rode back to the Broken Arrow Ranch. Pat and I were thick as thieves since she answered the phone a few nights ago. It was her idea that I come and stay in a cabin at the ranch while my sale closed. It was her idea that I spend as much time as I wanted with them, free of charge. And, it was her idea to not tell Rhett I was coming.

"He's as lovesick as it gets, dear. I want to tell him; I do. But right now, he's experiencing a few days of growth that he desperately needed. Just today, in fact, the movie producers are recording one of his songs for the soundtrack. He wouldn't have ever done anything like that before he met you. You brought him out of his shell, and now he's finding out who he really is." I was so excited to hear that his music would be part of the movie. As I rattled off questions about it, Pat answered them in rapid-fire. I had one more question when we were done.

"Will seeing me put all of this growth to a halt?" I asked, half smiling. She shook her head.

"No, I don't think so. You are the reason for the growth, Sadie. I know my son, and you are the reason for all of this. We couldn't be more excited about you two liking each other." My cheeks reddened at the simplicity of the thought that Rhett liked me. Gorgeous, masculine, handsome as heck Rhett liked me. I couldn't wait to be back.

Finally, we pulled up to the ranch. At first, I joked that nothing had changed in the few days I had been gone. I was going to thank her for keeping everything as I'd left it, when I looked over at my cabin and saw a huge crew carrying out parts and pieces. Among all of the men, there was one with his back to me when I got out of the truck.

Pat smiled and nodded, motioning that I should go. "I'll get the luggage," she said with a wink. I kept my eyes on the guy, his broad shoulders towering over the men around him. He was wearing that dirty brown cowboy hat. His regular, worn jeans. The familiarity of his silhouette made me weak in the knees. He was frozen still as I clomped my sandals towards him. Finally, I was right behind him, just waiting for him to turn around.

"What, did I sneak up on you? In shoes like *these?*" His body was rigid at my words. Stiff. Immobilized. Slowly, he turned around, a shakiness to him. When his eyes met mine, he took me into his arms immediately, where he kept me tight in his embrace for what felt like forever

CHAPTER 32

Rhett

When we were done recording, hours had passed. Several parts of the song needed more than one take, so to speak, as Matt politely critiqued me. I found that I enjoyed the feedback, and I could see doing this again. I prayed that I could do this again. I really liked this whole experience—lending my music for a movie— something that would enhance Sadie's roles, and I was just the voice behind it.

Sadie. I could hear those footsteps in a crowded auditorium. I could sense her presence from miles away. And there was no mistaking the shoes that made sounds like that. There was no mistaking the woman who wore them.

"What, did I sneak up on you?" Her words sliced through the air like a knife. I'd never felt this level of relief in my life. I'd never praised God so much before this very second. "In shoes like *these?*" For a moment, I couldn't turn. I thought if I did, she would turn into a butterfly and disappear. It was irrational. It was insane. And then, I put all of that behind me and took her into my arms as fast as I could. I was back with the one that my soul loved, and I thanked God for the moment.

*****

It wasn't two weeks into Sadie being back before she closed on the land down the lane from here. Right next to the raccoon house, as I had called it in my head. Sadie had asked me to go with her to get the keys to the cabin, and I did. When we got there, we realized that was just a formality because the cabin would need to have a front door in order to have a key. We laughed and laughed at the dilapidated condition of the place, but Sadie let on that she knew the photos from the listing were outdated.

"Honestly, I don't care. Pat and I have it worked out that I can rent from the Broken Arrow until I have something livable built out here." I nodded, not surprised in the least.

"You two are thick as thieves, aren't you?" I teased, but not hiding the fact that I loved how close she was with my family. Sadie fit in like a missing piece.

"I'm in need of a strong man who can build me a cabin. Do you know of anyone?" Sadie asked as she pulled herself up and sat on the old kitchen counter of the shack. I shrugged. "Someone who has the strength to hold really heavy logs and stack them, just so?" I shrugged again, the smallest smile forming on my lips. She knew well that I had built my own cabin, and I could see where this was going. "Oh, I know! I'll call Molly's boyfriend. He knows how to build." She pulled out her phone, and I quickly plucked it out of her hand. From where she sat on the counter, we were at eye level, and we shared a kiss that rivaled all of the greatest love stories on earth, while I kept myself at a distance, so she wouldn't feel the ring box in my jacket pocket.

EPILOGUE

Sadie

One Year Later

"And the award for best actress in an independent film goes to...Sadie Clark!" The crowd cheered wildly as I stood, in my pink pantsuit with sparkle high heel shoes. The hunky cowboy beside me stood to give me a hug before I went off to accept an award for my role in *The Belle of Bitter Creek*, which turned out to be a smash hit. It got excellent ratings from viewers at home and better than expected from critics. It was picked up by two Christian movie networks, and one even did a limited movie theater release. The box office sales were enough for the production company to offer me two more films. After turning down *Gummy,* a decision that I assumed would be met with backlash, I was met with support from people looking for clean and uplifting content. There were more of them than I ever realized.

Now, as I held the award for something that I only could have done with God working through me, I thought back on my trials. How I was chewed up by Hollywood for a time—enough to see the true colors of some and the willingness of how far others would go to destroy you. The Lord led me through these trials with His promise of making things right for me. I didn't have to take revenge or set out to prove people wrong. He did all of that for me.

Standing at the podium, I thanked God for my blessings and opportunities. I thanked my parents, my manager Janie, and my best friend Molly. Lastly, I thanked my fiancé, Rhett Reed, for his unwavering support of my dreams.

After the awards show, Rhett and I skipped the parties and opted to have a nice dinner instead. We went to a quiet place that had tables stretched out far and wide, so people could still have privacy. In this part of Los Angeles, it wasn't uncommon to see actors and actresses everywhere, and places like this helped keep the feeling of normalcy in an otherwise different existence of strangers feeling like they knew you.

While we ate, we reflected on our short stay in California. It was no surprise that Rhett wasn't one for the big crowds. The longer I was in Wyoming, the more I wanted to be in Wyoming. We would be returning tomorrow, where he was just putting the finishing touches on our future home, and I was to be starring in a new role in another indie western right after our wedding next month.

The indie roles didn't pay nearly as much as the big blockbuster films, but the thing was, they paid enough. Enough to support my life in Wyoming. To make sure that my family had enough. To ensure my survival, with an occasional splurge, which was feeling a little more frequent these days, thanks to my new love of horseback riding.

After my movie was released, Tommy's show got cancelled. He hadn't been offered a job since, unfortunately. While I continued to pray for him, I thought of him less and less, as that part of my life was in the past, and someone whom I loved recently reminded me that God was in the present.

The next morning, as we met in the hallway of our hotel, his room next to mine, he handed me a hot coffee, took my bright pink suitcase along with his black one, and wheeled us out. We had a long travel day ahead of us, but no time spent with him was ever wasted. We truly enjoyed every moment together.

A few days later, back on my new land in Dust Creek, Rhett was finishing up the trim in the living room, the last room to be finished. Once he was done, and I was done taking pictures to send to my family, we went out and sat on the wrap around porch. It was a requirement that I had one, with two rocking chairs for the future rocking of babies.

There was a fresh pitcher of lemonade left on the porch by Pat, who had been here just a few minutes before. As we sipped the cold, icy beverage and looked out at the mountains, Rhett asked me what I was thinking.

"I don't think I'll ever get used to seeing raccoons run around in collars," I teased, as one skittered across the field in front of us.

"Ah, I think that's Tammy," Rhett said, his heart softening at the sight of her in her hot pink sweater. We laughed together that day, as I prayed we would for the rest of our lives.

With all of the glitz and the glamour in life, I'd been shown how easily all of it could fade away. But as long as you lived for the Lord and didn't follow the ways of the world, it didn't have to be perfect to be wonderful. True happiness came from

Jesus, and He would give you peace all the days of your life, if you let Him.

ABOUT THE AUTHOR

Cassandra discovered her passion for writing at the age of seven when she purchased a diary at the Scholastic Book Fair. What began with journal entries about her school and home life later evolved into a collection of poems, short stories, and novels. Her hobbies include skiing, traveling around the Rocky

Mountains, and reading. Much of her writing inspiration stems from her love of dogs, her Onondaga heritage, and her Christian faith. Cassandra's favorite genres of books are Christian fiction novels, Thrillers, and anything British.

She is a full-time writer and resides in the mountains of Wyoming with her husband, Chad.

Find her online at cassandrajoelle.com

OTHER BOOKS

A Ranger, A Wolf, and a Really Bad Tent: A Clean, No-Spice Christian Romcom

When her phone dies in Yellowstone, she just might find a real connection.

Ember Hollis is addicted to her phone and chasing relevance when a sudden microburst floods her Yellowstone campsite and waterlogs the one thing she can't live without. Forced offline, she collides with Ridge Sawyer: a rugged, very hot park ranger with cowboy roots, muscles for days, and no cell phone at all.

As the wilderness strips away the filters, Ember is forced to face herself. And while the park buzzes over a legendary wolf returning to Yellowstone for her mate, Ember discovers a deeper love—one that leads her not just to a man, but back to Christ.

Genre: Christian Romantic Comedy

Howdy, Handsome: An All-Space, No-Spice Christian Romcom

Houston, We Have A... Meet-Cute.

When a test flight goes sideways, astronaut Jack Carter crash-lands in the last place he expected: the middle of a Wyoming cattle ranch. Dazed, suffering from amnesia, and drop-dead handsome- he can't remember his mission- or even his own name.

Enter Annie McGraw, a cowgirl who doesn't have time for stray cattle... Let alone stray astronauts. But when she takes him in, sparks fly faster than a rocket launch. Out under Wyoming's star-filled skies, Jack launches into a mission he never trained for: a woman who just might be his greatest adventure yet, and a faith that grounds him more than gravity ever could.

Genre: Christian Romantic Comedy

The Chalet Next Door: An All-Ski, No-Spice Christian Romcom

Blizzard Outside. Banter Inside. Sparks Inevitable.

Bubbly book publisher Presley Astor has been told all her life she's "too much." But she's perfectly happy being herself- and taking her pampered Shih Tzu, Priscilla, on a solo ski trip to Sage Mountain, Wyoming. What she's not prepared for is a blizzard knocking out her power and forcing her to seek refuge in the chalet next door...with a brooding cowboy who clearly doesn't know what to do with someone like her. Ford Prescott is a guarded skijoring champion-a rodeo sport where a horse pulls a skier at breakneck speeds-preparing for the biggest race of his life. But he's also fighting cheating competitors and a faith that's quietly slipping through his fingers. As snow piles high and the town shuts down, Presley's joy (and Priscilla's undeniable charm) begins melting Ford's walls. But when old insecurities and misunderstandings hit harder than the storm, they'll have to decide if God's plan for them is bigger than just surviving the blizzard.

How to Fall for a Cowboy: An All-Pumpkin, No-Spice Christian Romcom

She's Glossy Nails. He's Flakey Crust. The Plan? Half-Baked.

In the town of Maple Haven, Wyoming, Autumn isn't just a season- it's a celebration. Ginger Hart is spending the season like she has for the past year: hopelessly crushing on Dallas, the gym bro who communicates in motivational quotes. In her quest for his attention, Ginger's lost more than a few pounds- maybe, a bit of herself. As the town gears up for the annual Pumpkin Stampede, something (or rather someone) rolls into town in a pumpkin-themed dessert truck parked right outside Ginger's salon. Behind the counter? Ex bull-rider Tucker Callahan. He's all cowboy hat and delicious sweets- basically everything Ginger's been trying to resist. When they decide to fake date for his image and for her to get Dallas' attention, he proposes one sugary-sweet condition. As cozy sparks fly, Ginger begins to wonder if God's sweetest plans aren't always the ones we bake up ourselves.

Genre: Christian Romantic Comedy

A Weather Girl's Guide to Love: A Thunderously Sweet Christian Romcom

Partly Cloudy, Mostly Complicated.

Hailey Sinclair had her life all mapped out- until God changed the forecast. Instead of being an on-air meteorologist for a national network, she's reporting the weather in rural Wyoming. Now she's caught between her college sweetheart, Jett Dawson, and Colt Wilder- the infuriatingly gorgeous and cheerful cameraman who seems determined to break through her stormy exterior. Torn between the future she planned, and the one God might be writing, Hailey must learn to trust His direction- and her heart- even when it leads straight into the eye of the storm.

Genre: Christian Romantic Comedy

A New Leash on Life: A Dog-Mom Rom-Com, Book 1

Get ready for a hilarious Christian romantic comedy as we follow the journey of a thirty-something introverted woman, Katie Fitzgerald, who's longing for a husband. But when she accidentally adopts a dog, she discovers that love comes in unexpected ways, and that God's timing is always perfect.

Genre: Christian Romantic Comedy

Fetching Love: A Dog-Mom Rom-Com, Book 2

Three couples, three journeys, and one hilarious adventure on the unpredictable path to love. Katie and Eli are ready to say "I do," but the days leading up to the wedding are full of surprises- especially when Katie's mom's true crime sleuthing lands her in a pickle. Samantha and Mitchell seem perfect together, but hidden struggles test their relationship. Can they find common ground, or will their opposing desires pull them apart? Carolyn and Micah have found faith and each other, but their surprise romance leads to a sudden, life- altering decision. As these couples follow the Lord, they find joy and laughter along the way.

Genre: Christian Romantic Comedy

The Après-Ski Proposal: A Romcom About Love Off-Piste

She came for a fresh start... Not a fake boyfriend. When Claire Riley gets dumped on the eve of her 30th birthday, she's blindsided. A spur-of-the-moment ski trip seems like the perfect escape, until she runs into her ex... With his new girlfriend. Shocked and desperate for a lifeline, Claire accepts a proposal from a charming stranger to pose as her fake- boyfriend. What begins as a simple act of saving face turns into a journey that reveals a fresh start in life and love—the kind that only God could have planned.

Genre: Christian Romantic Comedy

The Curse of Josephine Bagley

Over the course of a century, three individuals are woven together by a decades-old curse:

William, after surviving an Indian raid on his orphanage due to his facial disfigurement, goes on to live among the tribe. But when misfortune befalls them, he is quickly traded away and faced with a pivotal choice that changes his life forever.

Josephine has faced immense loss. Despite her granddaughter's efforts to help her find solace in faith, she finds she can't let go of the past and falls further into her belief that she's eternally bound to darkness.

Saraphina, a fledgling antiques dealer, gets the surprise of her life when a courier delivers notice that she's the last surviving relative of the Bagley Estate. What seemed like a windfall that could help her career now causes her to question her own reality.

In this tale of intertwining mystery, loss, and faith, these souls navigate through nefarious trials to find the gift of grace and forgiveness that extends to us all.

Genre: Christian Gothic